LUCKY GIRL

PAGE STREET
PUBLISHING CO.

PAGE STREET
PUBLISHING CO.

Distributed by Macmillan, sales in Canada by The Canadian Manda Group.

25   24   23   22   21   1   2   3   4   5

ISBN-13: 978-1-64567-208-1
ISBN-10: 1-64567-208-5

Library of Congress Control Number: 2020945238

Cover and book design by Laura Benton for Page Street Publishing Co.
Cover illustration by Mina Price

Printed and bound in the United States

FOR EVERYONE WHO COULD USE A LITTLE LUCK RIGHT NOW.

AND FOR ASHLEIGH, NOELLE, AND LIZZY—
THANK YOU FOR ALWAYS SHOWING UP.
I'M SO LUCKY TO HAVE YOU AS FRIENDS.

CHAPTER ONE

WHAT DO MOST PEOPLE DO WHEN THEY FIND OUT THEY'VE WON THE lottery?

Cry? Scream? Jump up and down? Quit their jobs? Call their moms or their best friends?

Or, fun alternate version to all that, they could take my approach and be sitting quietly in math class, chewing on their bottom lip, and trying not to faint.

Hi, yes. My name is Fortuna Jane Belleweather. I'm seventeen, and I've just found out I was the sole winner in last night's huge lotto jackpot. Like, $58 million worth of huge.

I'm freaking out, to say the least.

And look, okay. I get it.

Nobody feels sorry for lottery winners. I mean, it's hard to have sympathy for someone who can potentially make all their problems disappear with outrageous amounts of money.

BUT, as I'm quickly finding out, in the space between potential winner → to actual winner → to appearances on *Luxury Lotto Lifestyles*, there's a Pacific Ocean's worth of doubt, worry, and fear. There's also ample space for panic attacks like the one I'm having right now, in the middle of math class.

Outside my classroom's windows, a brisk October wind howls, making bare oak branches slap against the glass. Inside the classroom, I'm trying to breathe normally and stop my hands from shaking harder than the trees.

I'm failing spectacularly.

In fact, I'm pretty sure I'm about to start some deeply unhinged cackling soon, and I can feel the laugh sitting like a lump of unswallowed sandwich, stuck in that spot where my collarbones meet. Assuredly, hyena-style laughter during math class is a terrible idea, but at this point, I'll do anything to decrease the pressure of this absurd *$58 million–dollar* secret before my head actually explodes.

Deep breath in.

Hold it.

Deep breath out.

I count my breaths and think about numbers. Because numbers are concrete and make sense. There's strength in numbers, right?

Okay, here are some numbers:

For the last five years, my mom has played the lotto religiously.

Every week, she spends exactly forty-three dollars—a third of her check from working at Sammy's Storage Solutions—on lotto tickets. The rest of her check barely keeps us alive. Which is sort of fine because we live in the paid-off house Mom grew up in, and there's still some money left from my dad's life insurance.

But back to numbers: Multiply those forty-three dollars by fifty-two weeks, then multiply that by five years for a grand total of $11,180 that my mom has spent on the lotto since we moved to Lakesboro.

Which is probably only slightly more than what the guy in front of me in math class spent on hair gel last week.

Ha!

(More unhinged cackling. Breathe, woman. Breathe.)

Okay, right, the numbers. So, the amount of money I have in my pocket is approximately 5,245 times $11,180.

And now we're back to it: the $58 million—or, to be more precise, $58,642,129—I have in my pocket. During math class. On what started out as an ordinary Thursday.

All of which is absolutely, entirely, totally, mind-bogglingly absurd.

And which I also just found out about three minutes before class, when I popped into the bathroom to check the winning lotto numbers on my phone.

Yes, I nearly passed out on the toilet.

And no, I haven't told anyone yet. But I'm getting to that part.

To say I'm bewildered is like saying you should probably pack a sweater for a trip to Antarctica.

(HAHAHAHAHA. Jokes! At a time like this!)

Deep breath.

I think it's likely I'm in shock because I'm just sitting in class, all casual, with $58 MILLION IN MY POCKET.

But there you have it.

Last night, I impulsively bought a ticket with my last dollar. And it won.

I keep making myself say it in my mind: *I won the lottery.*

I won the lottery. I *won* the lottery. I won *the lottery*.

"Fortuna Jane Belleweather," calls out my math teacher, Ms. Wallace, peering at her attendance sheet. "Are you paying attention?"

Mr. Hairgel in front of me snickers. "Yeah, Tuna, are you paying attention?"

I poke him hard with a pencil eraser, which he probably thinks is flirting now that I'm single again. I've worked hard not to learn his name, since he also thinks my first name is the funniest thing he's ever heard. My mom thought naming me *Fortuna* was a smart bet for ensuring me a life of good luck. Maybe she was right, given my current lotto-winner status, but it also highlights how terrible her judgment is. Seriously. What kid ever wanted a name with the word *tuna* in it?

"It's Jane," I remind Ms. Wallace, who likes to deploy our full names as weapons. "And yes, I'm paying attention. We're talking about paramedics—I mean, ebolas—I mean, parabolas."

The class laughs. "Care to elaborate?" Ms. Wallace arches a perfectly drawn eyebrow.

"Fourteen," hisses my best friend, Brandon Kim, from the seat behind me. "The curve of that parabola is fourteen."

I repeat what he says, and Ms. Wallace goes back to her droning lesson. I whisper thanks to Bran and go back to feeling like Charlie goddamn Bucket with a pale-orange Mega-Wins ticket burning a Bentley-size hole in my pocket.

I still can't believe I won. I mean, what are the odds of that?

Actually, I know the odds because I've been covertly Googling since the start of class. There was a one in three hundred million chance I would be the sole winner of last night's jackpot.

That's right. One in three hundred million.

Also—according to Google—it's more likely I'd date a supermodel, get hit by an asteroid, achieve sainthood, and be eaten by a shark, all at the same time, rather than win the whole jackpot myself.

Which is something my brain refuses to wrap itself around. I keep thinking about it and then bouncing off the truth of my newfound wealth like a kid bopping around in a giant bounce house. Except it's a lot less fun. Maybe I'm like that kid who keeps falling out of the bounce house and landing on her face. Or the one who keeps slipping and getting pummeled by the other kids. Or whatever.

For perspective: Yesterday, I had twenty-four dollars in my bank account. Today, I have $58 million in my pocket.

To keep from having a full-blown panic attack, I doodle a picture of me and my supermodel date swimming in shark-infested waters while an asteroid races toward us. I make sure to include a halo over my head. Supermodel, shark, star, saint. Supermodel, shark, star, saint. The ridiculous combo runs through my head like a mantra.

Fun as that image is, though, my hand shakes as I sketch, sending a wobbly line across the page. I put down my pencil. Here are some other facts I've also learned since the start of math class:

Fact One: Lottery tickets are bearer's instruments. So, if I want this money, I better make sure I sign this ticket so no one else can cash it.

Fact Two: Even if I sign it, I can't cash it yet because a minor in the state of Wisconsin can only cash a ticket if it was bought by an adult and given as a gift.

Fact Three: I don't turn eighteen for another two weeks. But that's not the big issue, since I have one hundred and eighty days to claim the—

"Holy shit!" bursts out Bran. His phone chirps with a series of texts, and everyone in the class spins around to look at him. Ms. Wallace stops writing on the whiteboard and turns around, glaring at us all.

"Is there something you'd like to share, Mr. Kim?"

"Yeah! My dad just texted me—Wanda's Quick-Go Shop sold the winning Mega-Wins ticket last night. One person won the full prize of $58 million, and my dad says it could be somebody in town!"

Our town is right off the interstate, and Wanda's is one of two convenience stores, so there's a chance it could've been bought by anyone passing through.

But it wasn't, of course.

I shift lower in my seat, making sure the ticket is deep in my jeans pocket. I'm going to have to figure out a better solution for keeping it safe, but I certainly can't pull it out and shove it into my backpack right now.

Everyone in the class starts murmuring. Mr. Hairgel—who is newly eighteen—tells the girl next to him that he bought ten Mega-Wins tickets at Wanda's last night. I cringe to think of what he'd spend the prize money on if he had won. Probably a lifetime supply of hair products and dude-bro body spray.

All around me, phones come out, and everyone begins texting. Ms. Wallace starts to say something about putting phones away, but then she throws up her hands.

"Has anyone claimed the prize yet?" she asks Bran.

"Not yet. My dad says news crews are probably coming in tonight. They're going to interview people in town to see if they know anything."

My hand slips inside my pocket, and I run my fingers lightly over the winning ticket again.

It's all about numbers.

And last night they called mine: 6 28 19 30 82.

But considering the fever pitch the classroom has now reached, I'm not sure this is my lucky day after all.

CHAPTER TWO

O R MAYBE IT IS. I DON'T KNOW.

One part of me says: *Jane, you big dork. Winning the lotto is marvelous. Stop worrying so much; you'll figure it out. THIS IS GOING TO CHANGE YOUR LIFE IN AMAZING WAYS.*

Sure, right, says my more cynical side. *This is clearly too good to be true. Don't get your hopes up; something will go terribly wrong.*

I war with myself for the rest of the morning, feeling deeply conflicted about the whole thing. I have more lotto-winner research to do, which I'm saving for tonight, when I'm at home and not surrounded by hordes of people talking about the ticket and what they'd do with the money.

By lunchtime, the news of the winning ticket has spread throughout the school. Facebook, Instagram, Twitter, and Snapchat are all buzzing. Half the school is checking their phones to see if they know the winner, and the other half is posting pictures for the impromptu "Where were you when you found out about the ticket?" selfie stream on Instagram that some industrious soul thought was a good idea.

Bran is offering tidbits of lottery information on his social media and his website, Bran's Lakesboro Daily. He started the site a few years ago as part of a class project, but since then it's grown from a small school newspaper to something that covers news for the whole town. Bran's a brilliant journalist, and he's hoping the site will help him get a CNN internship this summer and also help with college applications. When I last saw him, he was running an "Ask Me Anything" on Instagram and scrambling to keep up with questions from people at school.

I was following along for a while, but now I've turned off my phone, and I sit at a picnic table in the yard behind school, eating a ketchup sandwich and trying not to think about the ticket.

Which is about as easy as forgetting to breathe.

I pull apart my sandwich with a sigh. The blob of ketchup on the white bread looks like a bloodstain, but there was nothing else in the fridge this morning because Mom forgot to go grocery shopping again.

With a resigned bite (it tastes like chewing on salty tomato-flavored Styrofoam), I try to enjoy the weather. Leaves flutter down from the oaks above my head, though the wind carries the promise of bitterly cold winter days. Just the thought of waiting for the school bus on 20-degree mornings makes me want to crawl into a volcano.

I pull a ratty green sweatshirt out of my enamel-pin-covered backpack (*RBG! She persisted! Nasty Woman! Books!*) and slip it over my T-shirt. Then, with a glance over my shoulder to make sure no one is looking, I take the lotto ticket from my jeans pocket and tuck it between the pages of my favorite book, *Sea Change*, by legendary oceanographer Sylvia Earle.

Opening to a random chapter, my eyes move over Earle's words, but I'm not taking anything in. Usually when I read this book, I'm transported to my favorite place in the world that I've never actually been—the Hawaiian Islands Humpback Whale National Marine Sanctuary—but today I'm just reading the same sentence over and over.

Which is all because of this damn ticket. I shove it deeper into the book and close my eyes. If can't read, I'll just travel to Maui in my mind.

I'm on a boat off the coast. The deck rocks beneath me, and a salty breeze lifts my hair. Gulls screech and waves slap against the sides of the hull. Suddenly, something goes flying up from the deck—it's bright orange, and I grab for it.

No! That's a lotto ticket, and I'm trying to forget it for a moment. Taking a deep breath, I sink back into the fantasy of Maui.

Steadying myself, I scan the ocean for the enormous gray shape of a humpback whale. In the distance, Maui's green hills rise, and the sapphire-blue Pacific stretches to the horizon. Suddenly, there's a great rush of water—

"Uh-oh," says Bran from somewhere nearby. "You've got that 'dreaming about whale watching in Maui' look on your face again."

My eyes fly open, and I snap my book closed, making sure the Mega-Wins ticket isn't showing. I need to find a safer place for it. Like, immediately.

"If you were really my best friend, you'd know I'm daydreaming about working with Sylvia Earle *while* whale watching in Maui."

Bran rolls his eyes and plops down at the picnic table beside me. Today he's wearing a band T-shirt I found for him at a thrift store, ripped jeans, and sneakers. Whereas I just look messy in my sweatshirt and jeans, he somehow looks like a K-pop star who's wandered into rural Wisconsin.

Scowling at my very sad ketchup sandwich, Bran offers me a bag of grapes from his own lunch without a word. I take the grapes and shove *Sea Change* into my backpack.

Before Bran can say anything else, his phone rings. "It's Sofie," he says excitedly.

Sofie is Bran's long-distance girlfriend. She was an exchange student at our school last year, and she moved back to Sydney in May. Somehow, she and Bran have been making it work with half a continent and an ocean between them.

"Hi, Sof," I say as Bran answers the FaceTime call.

Sofie and I chat online frequently, but because of the time difference, we rarely manage to have an actual phone call.

Sofie grins at me. She's wearing green pj's with corgis on them, and her curly hair frames her light-brown face. "Jane!" she says. "So good to see you!"

I grin back. "What time is it there? Like, six in the morning?"

"Closer to four, but these are the things we do for love." Sofie sips from a giant mug of coffee.

I nudge Bran. "I hope she calls *you* at four o'clock in the morning too, just to keep things fair."

He laughs. "We're ridiculous, I know."

They take a minute to make googly eyes at each other, and Sofie blows Bran a kiss.

"You two are sickening." I groan.

"Admit it," Sofie says with a laugh. "You want to be awoken before dawn to chat with your beloved too."

I snort and run a hand over my eyes. "Not even a little bit. But I'm also not dating again until I'm thirty."

This resolution was formed after Holden Jones—the guy I dated since the beginning of sophomore year—suddenly broke up with me two months ago. Right now, I'm totally over love and romance. Give me humpback whales over making out any day of the week.

"You'll find the right person someday," says Bran, ever the romantic. Sofie nods in agreement on the screen. "Just think, the girl of your dreams could be waiting on your boat in Maui."

"Shut it," I say with a snort. I don't regret telling him that Megan Rapinoe lifting her hands in triumph in the World Cup against France confirmed my suspicions about being bi, but his optimism for my love life is just too much right now.

"How are you holding up, Jane?" Sofie asks. She pauses for a moment and then presses on. "Bran told me about Holden."

Oooof. That hurts a bit. Not that Bran told her, but the reminder that at this time last year, we were doing things like going on double dates.

"I've been better," I admit.

"I'm so angry at him," Sofie bursts out. "What was he thinking? Like, did you even see it coming?"

"Not even a little bit," I say, unable to keep the bitterness out of my voice. I don't say this, but I can't help thinking it: In my mind, Holden and I had been like a couple in a rom-com. He wooed me back in tenth grade by writing me a song and leaving me long letters in my locker. Even after we'd dated for a while, he'd bring me flowers every week. We always danced in the rain. I went on his family vacations, and, if I spent the night at his house, his mom would make me breakfast.

He was all my firsts: first boyfriend, first kiss, first love, first (and only) guy I've had sex with. First one to break my heart into pieces.

Sofie makes a sympathetic noise.

I go on. "I swear, he was fine until he went to that stupid Future Investor's Club of America camp in Manhattan last summer. He broke up with me the day he got home."

"But he gave you no reason why?" says Sofie.

An unwelcome tear rolls down my face. Dammit. I'm so tired of crying over Holden. "He said he wanted to experience the world and date other people, that I didn't see him for who he really was, and that I was holding him back. I thought he loved me, but—"

My voice breaks as I say it. Holden's admission that my love wasn't enough for him still hurts like a broken bone. I've had time to let it set, but there's a deep ache that marks how I've been changed.

How can love be there one moment and gone the next? Did I miss the signs? I still have no idea, and I hate that I'm still asking myself these questions two months later.

I mean, I'm a girl who likes puppies, dorky romantic movies, babysitting kids, reading until dawn, and laughing too loudly. Or I was that girl. Lately, I just feel like this sad sack of a human who can't get past an already-done relationship.

I'm so over feeling sad, but I can't quite get over Holden.

Ugh.

I bury my head in my hands and groan. "See my previous comment about not dating until I'm thirty."

"I'm sorry, Jane," says Sofie. "I wish I was there to give you a hug and throw eggs at Holden. Bran, hug Jane for me." She opens her arms like she's hugging me.

"You're a delight," I say, blowing her a kiss.

Bran gives me a hug, and I lean into it, grateful for his steady friendship and the fact that Sofie is cool with me being best friends with her boyfriend and that it's not weird between us when he does things like hug me.

"Okay, okay," says Bran, once he releases me from the hug. "Lunchtime is almost over; let's forget about the worst of all possible humans, Holden, and talk about the money."

"What money?" I ask, trying to sound casual and not give myself away. My voice quavers, though, as I say it, and I can't help but glimpse toward my backpack like an ax murderer who's trying not to reveal where the bodies are buried.

I can't show my friends the winning ticket because who knows how they'd react. The last thing I need is for them to get weird because I'm now worth $58 million.

"The lotto money, silly," says Sofie. "Bran texted me about it hours ago. Can you believe it? Somebody in your teeny-tiny town won millions of dollars!"

"I wonder who it is?" asks Bran, taking a bite of his sandwich.

Sofie shrugs. "Whoever it is, they're so lucky. If I had that much money, I'd drop out of school immediately and buy a villa in Europe."

"I'd use it to take you both somewhere really nice," says Bran. "Somewhere special like Cirque du Soleil in Las Vegas."

Sofie and I both crack up at the same time.

"If you had that much money," she says, "you'd take us on a vacation to the tropics, not Vegas."

"Fair point," says Bran. "If we're taking this vacation, I suppose I'd have to buy a private jet or something."

"You couldn't buy a private jet with that money," declares a smug voice from behind me.

I whip around, my body responding to that voice with a surge of loathing, lust, and lost-love ache that I'm still trying to untangle.

Holden Jones walks up to our table, hands in his pockets. Ever fashionable these days, he's wearing an Armani T-shirt, form-fitting jeans that make me want to weep a little, and a gray wool coat that likely cost more than a car payment. Since he got back from FICA (or, as I like to call it, *The Wolf of Wall Street*) camp, he's been reading *GQ* religiously and working extra hours at his dad's hardware store to buy expensive clothes.

Gross, right?

Not the designer clothes—because look good if you want, that's fine—but Holden's new stockbroker, dude-bro aspirations are too much. If he'd been like this when we were dating, I like to think I would've dumped him.

Even as that thought rises, I can't help but notice that despite how much he's changed, he's still gorgeous. Curse his stupid romance-novel-guy, shoulder-length black hair, his annoying deep-blue eyes, the not-adorable-at-all smattering of freckles across his cheeks, and his oh-so-familiar hands that know their way around my body so well.

He used to be funny. And smart. And kind.

And he used to make me feel different from anyone I've ever met.

And . . .

Ugh.

I think I hate him now almost as much as I thought I loved him. When he first joined Ecology Club two years ago, I thought I'd have to spend the entire time pretending not to like him. But then he was into me, and we were a thing. I miss being a part of us so much sometimes.

Holden scoots himself onto the picnic bench beside me, entirely too close for comfort. I bump him off.

"We broke up," I remind him. "I got the friend group in the divorce."

He laughs. "But you said, 'Let's stay friends,' so here I am, friend."

"Nope," I say, shoving him farther off the bench. "Go sit over there if you must." I point to the other side of the table.

Bran gives him a poisonous look, but onscreen, Sofie waves as Holden sits down. She's by far nicer than Bran and I combined.

"So," Holden continues, "as I was saying, you can't buy a private jet with $58 million. Or you could, but if you take a one-time payout, after taxes, you're looking at, like, thirty million dollars. Private jets start near ten million, so after you fill it with gas a few times, find a crew, and pay airport fees, I bet you could get from Madison to London and home again, and then you're out of money."

"How do you know that?" I ask. Apparently, this white-guy mansplaining is a part of Holden's new personality too. Fun.

"I looked it up," says Holden. "At FICA camp, my roommate's family had a private jet. He took me on it on the weekend when we flew from New York to Charleston to see his grandparents. After that, I researched all about how much it costs to have one, for when I've got my own someday."

I roll my eyes.

Bran and Sofie both start talking at once, arguing with Holden about the actual costs of owning a private jet. Which is hilarious, since we're all not-rich kids who are hoping for college scholarships.

"Hey!" says Sofie suddenly. "Jane didn't tell us what she'd do with the lotto money."

"Yeah," Holden chimes in. "What would you do with the money, Fortuna Jane?"

His eyes sparkle like the Pacific Ocean, and, I swear, I've never hated anyone so much. Seriously, in that moment when he uses my full name, I feel like a superhero whose nemesis has finally been revealed.

I tear my eyes away from his and fiddle with the strings of my hoodie. "Well, Holden Haden Jones——"

Bran snorts, and I shoot him a grateful look.

"I'm not sure what I'd do if I won that much money. I'm willing to bet winning the lottery brings nothing but trouble to the winners."

"That's true," says Bran. "Did you know there's something called the 'lottery winner's curse'?"

Everyone stares at him, and I file the information into my shit-to-look-up-later-about-the-lottery mental list.

Bran goes on. "I researched it this morning. A huge number of people who win the lotto actually end up brutally murdered by their loved ones."

"Well, that's depressing, Bran," says Sofie.

Holden fixes me with a look. "And Jane still didn't tell us what she'd do with the money if she won."

I think about the orange Mega-Wins ticket I'm using as a bookmark. What will I do with it? Besides hide it for the next two weeks until I'm old enough to cash it.

"I have no idea," I admit. It feels good to be honest about something today.

The bell rings, and Holden gets up without saying goodbye.

As he walks away, Sofie gives me a small smile. "I know you've got to go, but Jane, you should know, you can do so much better than Holden. And I'm here if you ever need to chat."

"I know I can," I agree. "And thank you."

Bran and Sofie say goodbye (promising to FaceTime each other later, when they have more privacy, eww).

Bran hangs up the phone, and we start to walk back toward school.

"You okay?" He's been asking me that nearly every minute of

every day since Holden dumped me. It's endearing and annoying in equal measure.

I shrug. "Totally fine. Just having a strange day because of this lotto stuff."

"I think the whole town feels your pain," says Bran. "See you at work tonight?"

I work at the pumpkin farm Bran's family owns. "I'm off tonight. Plus, it's a Big Junk Dump day tomorrow, so I'm sure you'll see me around town."

Big Junk Dump day (a painfully regrettable name, I know) or BJD day happens twice a month. It's a day where everyone hauls old TVs, high chairs, broken coffee tables, boxes, and everything in between to the curb. Lots of people will pick up the occasional item off the curb, but my mom—a woman who's made it her mission in life to save other people's memories—lives for Big Junk Dump day.

Tonight, Mom will force me into an evening of pawing through whatever's been left on the curb. Talk about a fun bonding activity. Or a way to up my high-school cool points. I mean, thanks to Mom, I actually got nominated last year as the future senior "Most Likely to Be Seen Going through Somebody Else's Trash." A sobriquet the yearbook editor vetoed, but still. What a claim to fame.

"Call me if you need anything tonight," Bran says. "Maybe we can get you out of BJD somehow." Bran has strong opinions about my mom, but he's also a good-enough friend not to get into them at school.

"You're a wonderful human—thank you." I smile at him and then the lunchtime warning bell rings. We only have two minutes before our next class.

"This ticket is going to change everything around here," Bran calls out over his shoulder as he rushes toward his class. "I can feel it!"

He's absolutely right. And I'm so ready for a change. Somehow, I'm going to cash this ticket, get my mom some help, take myself on a vacation, and get over Holden Jones at last.

CHAPTER THREE

THE REST OF THE DAY IS A BLUR. I MAKE IT THROUGH MY CLASSES and manage to remember the Ecology Club meeting after school. As I walk through halls filled with students still gossiping about the ticket, I keep my head down. It's all I can do not to shout, "I WON THE LOTTO! IT'S ME YOU'RE TALKING ABOUT! JUST STOP ALREADY."

What would the other students do if I did shout that? Call me a liar? Rip my backpack apart to find the ticket? What is it they say— we're all three days to becoming animals in disaster situations? How much more quickly do we descend when huge amounts of money are at stake?

"I wonder how anyone could keep this a secret?" says a blond girl in a Green Bay Packers sweatshirt. My school isn't huge, but I don't know her or her group of friends.

"Excuse me," I mutter, as I push through the knot of their bodies. They're all clustered by the water fountain and blocking the hallway.

All the girls stare at me, and one whispers, "That's her. Holden's ex."

As if I didn't have a name. For so long, I was known as "Holden's girlfriend" around school; now I'm destined to be "Holden's ex." Ugh.

"Why did he date her for so long?" The first girl's incredulous tone makes me want to hit her.

Because I'm funny, and cute, and smart, and really good at kissing, I want to shout. At least those are the things Holden used to tell me.

Honestly, though, I'm not even sure those things are true anymore. I mean, of course they are on some objective level, and my self-esteem isn't so low that I really think I'm worthless.

Fuck, though. Sometimes I struggle to remember who I am outside of the couple Holden and I were.

"I hate what she did with her hair," says another girl in the group.

I chopped off all my hair the night of the breakup, giving myself a horrifying mullet that Bran helped me fix by shaving my head. Two months later, it's still super short, and I adore it.

"Why did she even do that?" asks the first girl. "It's hideous."

I did it because Holden liked my long hair but not me anymore. And because I needed to feel like I was in control of something. And mostly because I always cut my hair when I want to scream.

I take a deep, steadying breath, come out of my morose thoughts, and turn around. "Oh, get a life," I say to the girl. "My hair is cute, and girls shouldn't bring other girls down like this. Life is hard enough for women. Don't make it worse by commenting negatively about every female body you see. Let me know if you want some book recommendations about that, and have a gorgeous day."

And flounce.

The girl's mouth drops open. I walk away, unable to stop the grin that spreads across my face as I head to my favorite place in the school: Mrs. Davis's biology classroom.

MRS. DAVIS'S CLASSROOM SMELLS LIKE WHITEBOARD MARKERS, SWEATY students, and a bit of biology funk that's decaying leaves with overtones of formaldehyde. Ecology Club starts in ten minutes, but the room is empty when I walk in—though I can hear Mrs. Davis in the teacher's office that's connected to the back of the classroom. Setting my backpack on the closest desk, I breathe in deeply, as if I can take the quiet and calm into myself, letting it fill me like water racing into a tide pool. To keep myself from stewing about Holden or the benightedness of some high-school girls, I focus on yesterday, when I bought the lotto ticket.

It's not like I intended to buy it when I walked into Wanda's Quick-Go Shop—or even thought I could. Sure, I'd tried to buy a ticket before at Wanda's, but Wanda or her wife, Mary Anne, always carded everyone who looked under eighteen. No exceptions. No questions asked. Those were the rules, and we all knew them.

Except yesterday was my dead dad's birthday *and* the two-month anniversary of Holden dumping me. So, no. I wasn't thinking of the rules. Or Wanda and Mary Anne. Or getting in trouble for buying a ticket. I was thinking about how in love my parents used to be. And how Mom, Dad, and I would go to my dad's favorite seafood restaurant every year on his birthday. And how I haven't eaten seafood since he died five years ago.

Knowing our fridge was probably empty at home, I'd stopped by Wanda's for an after-soccer-practice snack. I wore sweats, a hoodie emblazoned with our school mascot (Go, Honey Badgers!), and a light-pink jacket. I even had on my backpack, so I definitely looked like a student. But there was someone new working the counter at

Wanda's. It was some middle-aged guy who kept pressing the wrong button on the register. His face got redder with each messed-up transaction, and he swore under his breath.

"Sorry, sorry," he'd call out, as he mis-rang another item. "Work with me here; I'm new. Wanda is out running some errands. She'll be back soon."

As I shuffled forward in the long line of customers snaking through the store—some truck drivers, some parents with whining little kids, but no one from my school—I glanced up at the sign above the register: *Today's Jackpot: $58,642,129.*

That's a lot of money, I remember thinking. A ridiculous amount.

And then—and I'm about the least mystical person around, truly—I swear I had the clearest sense that I should buy a lotto ticket. Just one. Just because.

Maybe it was my dad nudging me from the Great Beyond. Maybe it was me wanting to break a rule. Whatever it was, when it was my turn to pay for my items, I stepped up to the register confidently.

"Is this all?" asked the flustered clerk. He didn't look up at me but gestured instead at my bag of pretzels, my juice, and the two frozen burritos on the counter (dinner for Mom and me).

"All this and a Mega-Wins ticket," I said, making my voice assured and breezy.

Still not looking at me, the clerk pushed some buttons on the lotto-ticket machine. It spit out an orange ticket. The clerk pushed the ticket across the counter toward me.

6 28 19 30 82.

I stared at the numbers on the ticket, feeling vaguely disappointed that I had a ticket with a bunch of random digits on it, when I could've done something symbolic, like played my dad's birthday—10/13/77—or his death day—8/17/16—or something else, but I didn't say anything because making a fuss might've made the clerk take a closer look at me. Or remember that minors weren't supposed to buy lotto tickets.

"That'll be nine dollars and ninety-two cents," said the clerk.

"Keep the change," I said, quickly handing over a ten-dollar bill and turning around with the lotto ticket still in my hand.

I stepped out of the way so a dad with a crying toddler in his arms could pay for his items, and then I stuffed all the food into my backpack. With one more glance at the ticket, I whispered under my breath, "Okay, universe. I bought a lotto ticket; let's see what comes next."

Never taunt the universe, right?

"Ahhh, Jane," says Mrs. Davis, walking into the biology classroom from her office. She's a spry woman in her early sixties. Today, she's wearing her customary socks and Birkenstocks, a T-shirt with wolves on it, and silver spiders dangle from her ears. She's totally old-lady-eco-warrior goals.

"Hi, Mrs. Davis," I say with a small smile. "How are you?"

"Damn tired of all these students not paying attention in my class because they're all abuzz about this lottery nonsense. How are you?"

I slump into one of the closest desks. "Just damn tired, if I'm being honest."

Mrs. Davis gives me a shrewd look. "Too much studying?"

I snort, then try to make it sound like a cough. "Yep, that's it."

I suspect she wants to ask me more about how things are at home, or to ask about Holden.

But she doesn't do either of those things, which is lovely of her.

"Are you ready for today's meeting?" Mrs. Davis asks as she starts gathering things from the back cabinets and hands me a stack of papers. "I've pulled some material that might help the newer members."

For a moment, I blank on what she's talking about. Then I remember: Right, we're supposed to be talking about water quality in the Great Lakes region and what we can do to help. I volunteered to discuss some of my own research on the oceans, as prep for our trip to Lake Michigan next month.

"Of course," I say, taking the papers. They're yellowish and held together with rusty staples. "I'm totally prepared. These should help."

"That's my girl," says Mrs. Davis fondly. She pats me on the back. "And don't forget our aquarium-store field trip tomorrow."

"I wouldn't miss it for the world," I say. (I'd totally forgotten it, but right, we're taking a bunch of third graders to an aquarium store in Madison tomorrow. Got it.)

"You're doing a great job as the club president, and I can't wait to see what the future holds for you. You have so much potential."

It's as close as Mrs. Davis gets to giving me a hug, and it buoys me immensely. Before I can thank her or even reply, she walks back toward her office. I try to gather my thoughts, desperately wondering what I'm going to say about the water quality of the Great Lakes, when all I can think about are fifty-eight million reasons to flee from the Ecology Club meeting before anyone else—especially Holden—gets there.

J. WILKINS: Hey, folks! I'm looking for a contractor who will replace the toilets in our house. Raccoons somehow found their way in . . . [20 more comments]

AMY PEMBERLY: OMG OMG! Did you all hear? The winning lotto ticket was sold in our town last night! Somebody is gonna be riiiichhh! [Kim Kardashian gif]

    MARY FULTON: No way! I hadn't heard this! Wonder if it's somebody in town, or someone passing through?

        AMY PEMBERLY: Probably somebody passing through, off the highway. But can you imagine if it was somebody in town?

        LISA HAWKINS: Maybe that's how we'll get our town swimming pool. LOL.

            MARY FULTON: No need for a swimming pool. We have a lake! Are you too good to swim in the lake?

                LISA HAWKINS: Sheesh. Chill out. We're not rehashing the "swim in the lake already, pools are for snobs" argument again on here. We're discussing the $58 million winner.

AMY PEMBERLY: Why would someone keep the money a secret? If it were me, I'd be shouting it from the rafters.

MARY FULTON: Maybe they don't know yet? It just was announced this morning.

LISA HAWKINS: Ha! You're telling me you wouldn't check the numbers first thing? That's what I always do.

[50 more comments]

MARY FULTON: Not to change subjects too much, but this cow wandered into my yard this morning. Anybody know who it belongs to? Seems friendly enough . . . [picture of enormous dairy cow happily eating grass by a swing set]

AMY PEMBERLY: How does one lose a cow? Only in Lakesboro, lol.

MARY FULTON: This is nothing! Did I tell you about the bear that came through my yard a few weeks ago?

J. WILKINS: That's our cow! Thank you! We'll be right over.

CHAPTER FOUR

HEAD STRAIGHT HOME AFTER ECOLOGY CLUB. I'M EXHAUSTED AND incredibly grateful I don't have to work tonight. Work means talking to people, trying to keep my secret from Bran, and worrying a lot. Tonight, I need my room and my bed so I can try to calm my racing thoughts, which are screaming at me: *You won the lotto, you won the lotto, you won the lotto.*

Quiet, brain.

I walked home this afternoon—skipping the bus and a ride from Bran—so I could escape the chatter about the lotto winner. But it's mostly impossible. I even popped onto the town's Facebook group, which I never do, to see what people were saying about the winner. Confirmed: Everyone is talking about this lotto ticket and the mysterious winner.

With every step, I hear the ongoing swell of voices that filled the school today: *"I wonder who it is?"*

"Here's what I'd do . . ."

"Can you imagine—$58 million?"

These comments circle in my head like a swarm of mosquitoes, each one stinging me slightly. I push all the thoughts and voices down as soon as I reach my house.

Ahhh, home sweet trash heap.

Mom and I live on the far side of town, where the neighborhoods trickle off and fields of corn and soybeans spread out like picnic blankets. Out here, the houses are at least a half mile apart, and red barns with painted quilt squares on them dot the landscape. My house was once part of my grandparents' eighty-acre farm, but Grandma sold most of the land when Grandpa died (which is how she could afford a condo in Madison). Now we only have the original farmhouse and a small yard neighbored by cornstalks on one side and barbed wire and cows on the other. Which is fine with me. I'm glad we don't have close neighbors to yell at us about the yard.

With a long sigh, I step through the garden gate of my house. Part of the fence—which might have been made of white pickets once but now looks more like a mouthful of dirty broken teeth—falls off as I gently close the gate. The entirety of my front yard is filled with children's play equipment. There's a busted metal swing set, which Mom got out of the trash recently. A twisty yellow slide leans against it, not attached to anything. Scattered over the rest of the dead grass and weed-filled flowerbeds are dozens of plastic toys, playhouses, toddler swings, and every other sort of outdoor play item in between. It looks like a daycare threw up out here, except everything is decidedly hazardous and unsafe for kids. Mom started collecting this stuff from garage sales at the beginning of the summer.

"Mom, this is junk," I'd said then, hoping to forestall a new obsession. "There's nothing personal or sentimental about it."

"Nonsense, Fortuna Jane," she replied, bustling past me with an armload of broken plastic dump trucks. "Children loved these things once. That means they're personal, and we should rescue them from being forgotten in a landfill somewhere."

The space under the umbrella of "things loved by a child once" is nearly infinite, but the space in our house is limited. Simply put, we don't have room for much more junk. But Mom wasn't concerned about that.

"But you don't even know who they belonged to!" I had protested.

"It doesn't matter. My job is to keep things from being forgotten. Your job is to help me." She put the toy trucks down near a water table that was filled with rotting leaves. Sighing, I helped her unload the rest of the stuff she'd managed to "rescue."

At least she hasn't brought the outdoor play stuff into the house yet.

I step over two sandboxes shaped like turtles piled on the front porch and shove my key into the front door.

Our old farmhouse has been in the family for three generations, and Mom was raised here. She moved away for college, met my dad, and they headed to Nashville for her to try to be a country singer.

But then five years ago, when I was twelve, my firefighter dad got caught in a huge blaze and didn't come home.

Mom was never the same. She sold her guitar, moved back into Grandma's house with me, and started buying things that reminded her of my dad. At first it was a few things—a sweater like he used to wear. Or a book that had been his favorite.

But one day, she came home from a consignment store with a mug that had a photo on it.

"LOOK AT THIS!" she'd said, storming into the kitchen where I was working my way through some math homework with Grandma's help.

"Hi, Mom," I said, not looking up.

She had plunked the mug down on the table in front of us.

"LOOK," she demanded.

I glanced up to see a picture of a redheaded kid in a soccer uniform staring back at me. *#1 SOCCER STAR!* was written across the top of the mug.

"Who's that?" I asked.

"I have no idea," said Mom quickly. "But that doesn't matter. How could someone throw this away? Imagine if you were that kid and you found out the mug with your picture on it had been given away like it was trash!"

Grandma and I shared a long look.

But we didn't say anything when Mom left the mug on a shelf in the living room.

"She's still grieving your father," said Grandma, so quietly that only I could hear her. "She'll get over this phase soon."

She didn't. Not even a little bit.

I push open the front door and flick on the light, knowing what awaits me inside: eyes. Thousands of them, staring at me from the mugs, T-shirts, and photos that fill our house. You know how they say the eyes on some paintings follow you? Well, multiply that feeling by a thousand and throw in a bunch of cheesy messages, and you'll have an approximate idea of how it feels to walk through my living room.

World's Best Dad!

#1 Grandma!

Baby's First Christmas!

The personalized items all shout at me from the bookshelves that line the walls and the piles Mom has made on the floor. I can no longer see the carpet, but there's a path among all the mounds of stuff. Perched on one pile is a half-eaten bowl of cereal—Mom must've had breakfast in here before she left for work. I gather it up and hurry into the kitchen, expertly navigating through the living room like a slalom skier.

The kitchen isn't much better than the living room, but thank God Mom doesn't hoard food. In fact, even when we have enough grocery money, she usually forgets to buy it, so that means I keep the fridge stocked with what I can, when I can. But every available inch of counter space is covered in more garage-sale and thrift-store finds. Most of this stuff isn't even personalized—Mom bought it because she thought we needed it or someone told her a story about it. Even if it's a pile of Big Gulp cups or a rusty can opener, she'll ask the person selling it if there's a story behind it. And if they don't tell her a story, she'll make up one about it.

She swears there's an organization to everything, but it's beyond me. All I can do is keep my own space clean and not mess with her stuff. Because she always knows when I do. If I were to throw away one of the four dish-drying racks piled on top of the stove, she'd know. Same with every other plastic cup, dented spoon, and piece of junk in the cabinets.

After stepping around a pair of high chairs that have appeared in the kitchen since I left for school this morning (apparently the nightmare-daycare mess *is* starting to enter the house), I rinse the cereal bowl and load it into the dishwasher, along with the other breakfast dishes I put in there earlier. Mom stopped cleaning years ago, and if I didn't pick up stuff, we'd have animals living among the piles of things. Well, we probably do, but not any that I can see.

Once I get the dishwasher going, I check the fridge—still empty of anything besides ketchup—and head to my room.

We used to have family portraits hanging on the walls going upstairs, but over the last few years, Mom has covered every inch of available space with other people's photos. It's still more strangers' eyes, cars, waving kids, and the million other things people take pictures of watching me trudge toward my room.

Upstairs, I squeeze past the pile of children's shoes that fills the second-floor hallway.

"Shit," I mutter as my backpack knocks some sneakers free. They cascade in front of me, and I trip over them. I throw out a hand to catch myself, but my shoulder slams into the bedroom door in the middle of the hall. The door swings open, and I slide into a mountain of stuffed animals.

This was Grandma's room. The one she had for sixty-five years, since she was born in this house. Now, none of Grandma's stuff is visible anymore, buried by the thousands of stuffed animals Mom has "rescued" for the sake of the kids who once loved them.

Shoving a mangy, orange stuffed kitten and a pair of eyeless teddy bears out of the way, I scramble to my feet. Somehow this room is even more full than it was a few weeks ago. Mercifully, Mom's not on to porcelain dolls yet, because of the expense. Just the thought of a room full of glass-eyed dolls makes me want to crawl out of my own skin.

Sighing, I kick a few more stuffed animals out of the way and pull the door shut. Once it's closed, there's a loud thumping as the stuffed animals resettle like shifting sands in the desert.

Grandma had the right idea moving out last year. "This place is too crowded for me," she'd said as she kissed my cheek. "But you can come stay with me any time."

I couldn't really. Because her apartment is on the Capitol Square in downtown Madison—"So close to the action, at last!" she likes to say—it's teeny tiny, and it takes half an hour to get there by car. Grandma asked me if I wanted to live with her, but I didn't want to leave my school, my friends, or Holden. And some part of me was afraid to leave Mom alone.

It occurs to me, all in a rush, that when I cash this lotto ticket,

I could buy Grandma a huge condo downtown. We could even be neighbors. I could probably buy the whole building.

And it's that thought that sends me tumbling over the edge, like I'm riding a tsunami made of stuffed animals and children's shoes.

A laugh rolls out of me, and once it's out, the jagged edges of panic, shock, worry, elation, and every other emotion I've bottled up today flow through me.

Chasing the laugh is a sob, and I struggle for a moment to haul air into my lungs.

I could buy a building.

Ridiculous.

With an effort, I push away all thoughts of Grandma or me suddenly becoming real estate tycoons.

The first thing I need to do is get to my room. The second is hide the ticket.

Everything else can come after that.

AFTER I UNLOCK MY BEDROOM DOOR USING THE KEY I KEEP ON MY KEY chain, something in me settles, just a little bit.

I always feel like Alice coming back from Wonderland when I cross into my room. Unlike every other chaotic space in the house, my room is clean, organized, and not filled to the brim with other people's garbage.

It's not fancy—there's a bed, a desk, my dresser, a closet with my clothes, and a small bathroom with a shower. But everything has a place. And everything is mine. The pictures of Bran and me on my bulletin board are tidy; there's the painting of the ocean Grandma made for me hanging above my bed; and on the other wall, above my desk, are framed maps of Hawaii and pictures of whales that I cut out from magazines a few years ago. My bookshelf is arranged by color, and it makes a rainbow on one wall.

I walk across the room, enjoying the fact that I don't have to dodge any piles of stuff or see any faces other than those of people I love. This is how a house should be. A place where people can live, not a place where stuff lives.

Dropping my backpack onto the floor, I flop onto my bed, exhausted by today.

But the ticket doesn't let me rest for long. It calls to me, like a living thing, tucked between the pages of my book. Rolling onto my stomach, I reach over the bed and pull *Sea Change* out of my bag.

The tiny orange-and-white ticket is still tucked in its pages, and it looks like it did when I bought it. Like it did before I knew what it was worth. Then, it was about potential. Now it's about so much else.

How could I be the one who won all this money? And what in the world am I going to do until I turn eighteen?

I mean, Mom has somehow managed to fill this house with a ton of junk—imagine what she could do with $58 million? She'd likely create a museum of precious things someone once loved, or something.

What do other lotto winners do with this much money? Or a better question: What does this much money do to them?

Shoving the ticket back into *Sea Change*, I pull out my phone and start researching lotto winners. I start with what Bran said at lunchtime.

"*Is there a lotto winner's curse?*" I type into Google.

The results are a resounding yes.

Clicking on the first article, I learn that over 70 percent of lotto winners end up broke in seven years or less. Or they end up dead.

Take example one: The Case of Abraham Shakespeare. (WHAT A NAME!)

In 2006, Abraham Shakespeare—an ex-con and high-school dropout—won $30 million (not much less than me when we're talking millions) in the Florida Lottery. Abraham was a nice guy. He shared his money with lots of people, but then he met Dee Dee Moore. By all accounts, Dee Dee was bad news from the start. She tricked Abraham into dating her, took control of his home, and bought herself a bunch of expensive stuff. Then, maybe she got tired of Abraham or maybe she wanted the money all to herself, but the short story is that Dee Dee killed Abraham and buried him under some concrete patio slabs in the backyard.

Talk about the death of romance!

But, wild as this tragic tale is, Abraham Shakespeare's story is not all that rare when it comes to lotto winners. In fact—

My phone rings, interrupting my Googling. It's Bran. The only person I know under seventy who still calls rather than texts. I almost don't pick up, but I can't let it go to voicemail. Because he'll keep calling.

"Hello?" My tone comes out more guarded than I expect.

"Jane." Bran's voice is intense. "Where are you? Are you sleeping? Are you okay? Why do you sound funny?"

"I'm fine. Just got home. Getting ready to start my homework."

"Don't do that. I know you're off tonight, but can you come to the farm? We're super slammed. Mom says she'll pay you for tonight's shift in cash."

"I don't know . . . I'm really—"

"Please. We need you, and it'll get you out of BJD day."

Right, I had almost forgotten about Big Junk Dump day.

"Excellent point . . ."

"Also, if you come to work, maybe we can find some time to talk about this lotto stuff. Have you seen my website or my social media? It's exploding with questions. Suddenly, I've become the expert on all things lotto."

The thought of him knowing so much about the lotto makes my insides squirm. But all I say is, "That's because you're the guy with the news in Lakesboro."

Bran laughs at that. "Possibly true, and you should check it out when you have a chance. Some of these questions are wild. So, what do you say? Come to the farm? I'll buy you a caramel apple and some coffee . . ."

My kryptonite. Of course I would say yes anyway, because I love Bran and his family, but throw in coffee and caramel apples? I'm powerless to resist.

I take a deep breath and let it out slowly. "Okay. I'll be there soon."

"Thank you, Janey. You're the greatest best friend ever." Bran's voice carries the smile I know is on his face.

"I know," I say as I hang up. But I'm pretty sure I'm not the best friend ever. I suspect that person wouldn't be hiding the fact that she won $58 million from her best friend. That person would be thinking of group vacations they could go on and planning on buying her BFF a car or something.

I shove those thoughts away as fiercely as I shove the book with the winning ticket into its slot on my bookshelf. There. Now *Sea Change* is just another blue book on the rainbow shelf. Nothing to mark it as special. And I can figure out whether or not I want to tell Bran more later, when I've wrapped my head around all this lotto stuff.

Is the ticket safe on my bookshelf, though? I pause for a moment, looking around my room. I think so? I mean, who would think to take it?

Thanks to a strict house rule and the lock on my door, Mom doesn't come into my room, and the odds of her knowing that *Sea Change* is my favorite book are slim, so it should be safe.

Then again, perhaps her knowing that is about as slim as the odds of me winning the lotto. *How'd that work out?* whispers a little voice in my head.

Before I can change my mind—I can't be hauling this ticket around all over town; what if I lose it?—I grab my backpack and head back into the tornado that is the rest of my house.

I'M SHUTTING THE FRONT DOOR WHEN MOM'S TRUCK PULLS INTO THE driveway. Heaps of stuff stick out of it at odd angles.

Mom clearly left work early to get started on her BJD pickups.

"Fortuna!" she says when she sees me. "Just the girl I was looking for!"

I got Dad's light-gray eyes and brown hair, but Mom and I have the same blindingly pale skin and short stature. That's where our resemblance ends. Mom hasn't had a haircut since dad died—I guess she's been collecting hair too—and it's so long that even when in a gray-blond ponytail, it falls past the back pockets of her jeans. She wears a *Doctor Who* T-shirt (one of Dad's) and work boots. She's painfully thin, but her face is completely made up. Like, full country singer/Dolly Parton contoured, with false lashes and everything else in between, because Mom won't be seen around town "without her face on." Though she will be seen around town gathering garbage.

I know. It's a mystery to me too.

I untangle my bike from the piles of broken toys that surround it. "Hi, Mom."

"Where are you headed?" she asks as I push the bike over to the side of the truck.

"To the pumpkin farm . . ."

"C'mon, Jane. You can't go now. We have stuff to pick up."

She says it like it's the most natural activity for a mother and daughter to do together. Like everyone in town won't be staring out their windows as we rifle through the trash they've left on the curb.

"Mom. I have to go to work; they're super busy and need me. I'll be back soon though," I say. I'm too tired for an argument.

"Can you help me unload at least?" Mom asks, gesturing toward the truck.

I check my phone. It'll take me half an hour to get to Bran's farm, but Mom is not one to let the junk stay in the truck. If I leave, it'll sit there, niggling at her, like an itch she can't scratch. She'll probably try to unload it and then hurt her back again, which barely slowed her down last Big Junk Dump day.

"I can give you ten minutes." I rest my bike against a tree.

Mom lets out a cheer and clambers into the back of the truck. "You're not going to believe what I found!" She throws down a life-size plush Siberian tiger that nearly knocks me over. "Can you believe someone threw that out?"

I can. Its white fur is now mossy green with mildew, and it's missing both eyes. It's the stuff of nightmares and will likely be placed in the middle of my living room.

"Totally unbelievable," I mutter under my breath as Mom flings another pile of stuff in my direction.

Eventually, the truck bed is empty. All the stuff is in the yard, and Mom is gleefully taking armfuls into the house.

"I'm leaving," I call out as she bangs through the screen door again and comes down the porch steps toward the yard. "We're out of food!"

She makes a noncommittal noise and gathers more stuff in her arms. "Get back soon, Jane! We still have lots more to rescue."

Of course we do. She's already headed back inside before I can reply. Suddenly delighted to get away from home for a while, I hop onto my bike and peddle as fast as I can toward Bran's family's pumpkin farm.

[Picture of Bran sitting on the Kim family pumpkin farm's giant rocking chair, grinning and holding a sign that says: LOTTO FUN FACTS!]

CAPTION: Hi lucky, wannabe lotto winners! Brandon Kim here with all your lotto questions answered! (For articles and more, check out my news site: Bran's Lakesboro Daily. Link in my bio.)

So, here's a lotto fact that no one's asked about yet, but I wanted to share:

Did you know that if a minor does (somehow) buy a lotto ticket in Wisconsin, they can't cash it, even after they turn eighteen? It's true. (In the US, that is. If you bought a ticket in the UK, it's totally fair game if you're at least sixteen.) But yeah, if the lotto commission finds out you bought it as a minor, then the prize is forfeit AND both the seller and the person who bought the ticket as a minor are guilty of a misdemeanor. So, hope none of you high-schoolers under eighteen bought a ticket. Lol!

Keep those questions coming, and I'll have more lotto updates later tonight.

#luckywinner #lottofacts #askmeanything #brandonkiminvestigates #themoreyouknow #allthelottoquestions #smalltownbigwinner

CHAPTER FIVE

AND SUDDENLY, I HAVE A NEW PROBLEM. AN ENORMOUS ONE.

An I'm-actually-a-criminal-if-I-cash-this-lotto-ticket-size problem.

Shit. Shit. Shit.

I'm standing outside the Kim family pumpkin farm, holding my phone in my trembling hand.

Loud, shrill giggles from the children's area split the evening, and there's a bonfire going near the back of the farm, which perfumes the air with wood smoke. I take a deep breath and read Bran's latest Instagram post again.

. . . if the lotto commission finds out you bought it as a minor, then the prize is forfeit AND both the seller and the person who bought the ticket as a minor are guilty of a misdemeanor.

Shit.

What am I going to do?

I can figure this out.

I think. Maybe? Possibly?

I pull my sweatshirt hood closer to my head as a brisk wind whips over me. Not far from where I'm standing, a pair of elementary-school-age kids run through the pumpkin patch, weaving around the hundreds of orange lumps within it. I envy their carefree joy. Imagine if my biggest problem tonight was deciding which pumpkin I wanted to take home?

Maybe there's a way around this rule? A loophole or something?

I read Bran's post a third time, biting one of my nails as I stare at the colorful pumpkin-farm sign.

"What should I do?" I say out loud.

The hand-painted pumpkins, skeletons in sunglasses, cornstalks wearing cowboy hats, and unicorns dressed as zombies on the sign are all resoundingly quiet on the issue.

I am so screwed.

How could I have missed this tiny, little MOST IMPORTANT FACT on my list of facts about the lotto? And why didn't I do more research? I've known about the winning ticket for hours. You'd think I'd have stumbled over this crucial piece of information by now.

But there was so much going on at school, and I didn't get enough time to research because Bran called me into work and then I ran into Mom, and HOLY SHIT. Am I going to jail?

Am I guilty of a misdemeanor? What does that even mean?

Further: I CAN'T BELIEVE I CAN'T CASH THIS TICKET WHEN I TURN EIGHTEEN. WHAT'S EVEN THE POINT OF TRYING?

Shit.

I don't want to give up all this money.

I really don't.

But what can I do?

Bran's mom spots me lurking by the pumpkin-farm sign. She gestures at me to come on up to the barn.

I wave to her, trying to imagine what it'd be like to be a part of

Bran's family. His grandparents bought this farm years ago when they moved to the US from South Korea (they were great friends with my grandparents, and there are stories about all the parties the four of them used to throw back when Bran's dad and my mom were growing up). Now that Bran's grandparents have retired to Florida, Bran's parents run the farm. His dad's an outdoorsy guy who loves everything about farming. His mom is a part-time children's book illustrator, and she also plays in an all-moms punk-rock band (Betty and the Killjoys, bless them). Basically, she's the coolest mom ever. Her sense of humor is all over the pumpkin farm, including in this year's corn-maze theme: outer space cats vs. aliens.

Yes, that means exactly what it sounds like; catstronauts in spaceships, battling aliens, are carved into the cornstalks. It's pure genius when seen from aerial photographs.

Families come from all over the state to visit the pumpkin farm and tonight, it's full of people. As I watch clumps of families and teenagers move through the pumpkin farm, I rack my brain for an idea of what to do with this lotto ticket.

People. Persons. One person. A person who is at least eighteen . . .

Ahhhh. There it is. An idea.

This is what I need to do: I have to find a person who's at least eighteen who will say they bought the lotto ticket; let them cash it; and then they can give me the money.

Sure sounds easy, but who do I know who could do it? If I were Bran, I'd ask my mom, and it would be fine. But I'm not Bran, and I can't even imagine what my mom would do with that much money. We'd likely have a whole castle full of other people's questionable photo-based gift choices. No, thank you.

So, okay, I can't ask Mom.

But can I really give up $58 million?

43

Of course I can't.

I've just got to find a way to get the money that doesn't involve my mom becoming a millionaire or me going to jail. And that means finding someone else who—

"Hey, you okay?" Bran says as he walks up to me and pulls me out of my thoughts. He's wearing an orange-and-black-striped apron over his clothes, and he has his pumpkin-shaped nametag on.

I am absolutely not okay.

"Yeah, I'm fine," I say, closing Instagram and shoving my phone into my pocket. "I was just heading in. Holy catstronauts, it's busy out here."

Bran laughs. "I know."

"Are you offering free hayrides or something?" I say as we walk through the parking lot. I chain my bike up outside the gift shop.

In addition to the corn maze and pumpkin patch, the Kim family pumpkin farm has a barn for making crafts, an awesome playground, and a snack stand that sells cider, caramel apples, hot dogs, and cotton candy. Tonight, every table in the outdoor eating area is full, kids scream with glee from the bounce house, and lots of couples walk around drinking steaming cups of cider.

Bran shakes his head, leaning against an antique farm wagon filled with pumpkins. "It's the time of year. Everybody just wants to be out and doing something before winter hits."

"It's definitely perfect pumpkin-patch weather," I say.

And it is. The air is crisp and cool. If I could bottle autumn in the heartland, it would look like this: twilight in mid-October at a Wisconsin pumpkin farm. I take a deep breath, inhaling the wood smoke and the hint of cold weather on the wind. It's immensely calming.

I could just ask Bran about his latest Instagram post. Or see if he knows any loopholes for criminal teens who bought lotto tickets that against all odds happened to win. Maybe I'll ask him anonymously later.

(I won't. I don't want to plant that idea in anyone's head.)

Before I can say anything else, a news van pulls into one of the parking spots near the gift shop. A young female reporter wearing a flannel shirt, leggings, and tall rain boots hops out of the front seat, looks around the farm, and walks over to us, microphone in hand.

"Excuse me," she calls out. "You work here, right?" She gestures toward Bran's apron and nametag. He nods. The reporter continues, "Can you point me in the direction of the owners of the farm? We're hoping to do a segment about the lotto winner."

Bran stands up a little taller. "This is my family's farm. I'm Brandon Kim, and we're happy to let you film here."

The reporter pauses for a moment, as if she's trying to figure out if she should ask someone else for permission, but she shrugs. "Good enough for me. We'll set up near the corn maze."

"Can I be on air?" Bran asks, his voice tinged with excitement.

The reporter nods as she's waving to the camera guy, who's walking toward her. "Sure thing. Just find me in about ten minutes when we're all set up. I'll put you on first."

Once the reporter has walked away, Bran grips my arm. "Yes! This is great. I can put this clip on my website and use it for my CNN internship application."

"Are you sure your parents are okay with this?" I ask, gesturing toward the news van.

Bran nods. "They expected some news coverage because the lotto winner is such a big story. And we're so busy tonight, they told me to keep an eye out."

"If you say so."

"How do I look?" he asks, taking off his orange-and-black apron.

I take a moment to appraise him. Under his apron, he wears boots, jeans, a T-shirt, and a vintage suit jacket that's somehow tailored perfectly. Out of nowhere, a grey fedora with a black hatband has appeared on his head. The look is somehow both stylish and also film noir detective, and I half expect him to drop into a weird 1930s accent and start smoking while drinking whiskey.

"Nice fedora." I snatch it off his head and plop it onto my own. "Where did that even come from? Are you hiding spare hats around the farm in case you need one?"

Bran snorts and grabs it back. "I had it on the wagon. And no fedora jokes, remember?"

I groan. "I still can't believe I lost that bet. Can I make just one fedora joke? Please?"

Bran shakes his head. "You knew the stakes when you agreed to guess the weight of the great pumpkin last year. Since I won—and let me remind you, your guess was off by an astonishing fifty pounds—I have clearly earned a year without fedora jokes. You promised."

The only excuse I have for such a sentence even leaving his mouth is that Bran went through a truly alarming fedora phase last year and doing things like guessing the weight of oversize pumpkins is how we entertain ourselves during the long (usually slow) hours as seasonal pumpkin-farm employees in rural Wisconsin. If I'd gotten the closer guess for the weight of last year's great pumpkin, Bran would've had to watch a new ocean documentary with me every weekend for the year. His loss.

"Year is almost up," I say. "Expect a rain of fedora jokes in approximately two weeks." Bran's mostly over the fedora phase (thank goodness), but I've been saving up jokes for months. They will have to come out eventually.

"I'd expect nothing less," says Bran. He adjusts his jacket and stands up taller. "But seriously, how do I look?"

"Minus the fedora?"

"Oh my God, you're such an ass," says Bran affectionately. He shoves me slightly, and I push him back, which draws a glare from a pair of moms pulling some toddlers in little red wagons.

"I'm just kidding," I say. "You look truly dashing and news ready. So, what's the plan for tonight?"

Bran shrugs. "I'm just going to play it by ear. See what their questions are. But I think I've figured out how to find the lucky winner."

And just like that, my stomach plummets like a pumpkin shot out of the pumpkin-chuckin' cannon.

It's one thing for Bran to be offering random lotto tidbits on his website and social media. It's another for him to be investigating it himself.

For a moment I want to just blurt out my secret and tell Bran I'm the one everyone is looking for. But with this new complication of not being able to cash in the ticket and perhaps being guilty of a misdemeanor, I need time to think before I tell anyone anything.

"Abraham Shakespeare," I whisper under my breath.

"What?" asks Bran.

"Just reminding myself of something," I say. And that's exactly it. Abraham Shakespeare was generous with his money. He told everyone about it. And he ended up buried under a concrete slab for his kindness.

Not that I think anyone in town will do me harm, but a lot of money makes a lot of people do strange things. Even in a town as seemingly wholesome as mine.

"So, how are you going to find the lucky winner?" I casually ask

Bran as we walk toward the news van. There's already a crowd of people there, making a semicircle around the reporter.

"You'll see," says Bran. "You want to be interviewed with me?"

I shake my head. "Uh-uh. Nope. No way. I'm terrible on camera. You know this."

"Jane, just because you're the queen of bad selfies doesn't mean you can't be on the news with me for ten seconds."

"My selfies aren't that bad, but there's absolutely no reason for me to be on camera with you. I'll be standing to the side cheering you on."

Plus, if I'm on camera, I might accidentally blurt out something about being the lotto winner.

"Okay. That works for me. Let's go."

Before I can say anything else, Bran's mom walks up to us. She's a fortysomething Korean woman who looks just like Bran. Tonight, her long black hair is pulled back into a stylish bun, but she's also wearing a Betty and the Killjoys T-shirt, so her tattoos are visible.

"There you are, Jane!" she says in a frazzled voice. She has a bag of kettle corn in one hand and a mug of cider in the other. "Thanks for coming in tonight. I'll need you in the gift shop eventually, but can you work the snack bar for half an hour while I sneak off for my dinner?"

"I definitely can," I say. "But I promised Bran I'd be moral support while he's interviewed. So give me like ten minutes?"

Quickly, Bran explains to his mom about the news van, how they're going to interview him, and how that will help with his internship.

"Are you sure Jane needs to be there?" asks Mrs. Kim.

"I really do," I say to her. "But it'll be quick."

Besides being moral support, I have some vague idea that me being there will keep Bran from getting too close to my secret.

Mrs. Kim takes a sip of her cider. "Fine, fine. Both of you just meet me at the snack bar when you're done. And, Bran, good luck." She straightens his fedora, which is both endearing and somehow so perfectly momish. Could I love either of these two humans more?

Bran grins excitedly, like he's about to go to a birthday party. This boy was made to be in front of a camera.

"I think I have a mom crush on your mother," I say as she walks away. "Want to trade?"

Bran rolls his eyes. "She's amazing, I know. We've been over this. But c'mon. They're about to get started." He strides away toward the news van, practically skipping.

I DON'T KNOW HOW HE'S DONE IT, BUT SOMEHOW IN THE THREE seconds it takes me to jog after him, Bran's already chatting with the reporter. He has a megawatt smile on his face, and she's laughing at something he's saying. He's so good at talking to people and being charismatic. Not for the first time, I wonder what he sees in me, a girl who would much rather spend her days alone on the ocean studying marine animals than doing anything even remotely cool.

"Ahhh, and this is my best friend, Jane Belleweather," says Bran as I walk up.

"Let's get rolling," says the reporter after a quick nod in my direction. She fluffs her hair once, and I step out of the way so I'm out of the shot. A light flicks on from the cameraman's camera. He counts down, three . . . two . . . one, and then waves a hand.

"Hello," says the reporter in a cheerfully enthusiastic voice.

"I'm Molly Rawlings, and this is WGN14 news. Tonight I travel to Lakesboro, a small town outside of Madison, where the winning Mega-Wins ticket was sold yesterday. As of five minutes ago, no one has come forward to claim the prize. I'm here at the Kim family pumpkin farm to talk with local residents to see what they think of this stroke of good luck and ask if they have any idea who the lucky winner is. First up, we'll talk to local teenager Brandon Kim."

Sweat beads my forehead, and I'm sure I look like a corpse who's been playing in a sprinkler. I hate that everyone is talking about this, and I hate that I haven't told Bran my secret, and frankly, I just want to run to the snack bar and hide. But a crowd has gathered around us, and there's no way I can push through them and flee into the night.

"So, where were you when the ticket was bought?" asks Molly.

"I was at home, catching up on some homework," Bran says. "It was pretty much just a normal day."

The reporter asks a few more questions, all of which Bran handles with ease.

Then, unexpectedly, Molly Rawlings turns her camera and microphone on me.

"This is another local teenager, Jane Belleweather," she says. "Jane, why do you think no one has come forward to claim the prize?"

"Maybe they're scared," I manage to choke out. Stage fright and a sense that everyone can see my secret makes my voice shake. "It could be a lot of pressure on them."

Molly gives an effortless laugh. "But it's a LOT of money. Surely that's worth a bit of pressure."

"I wish I'd won it!" someone calls out from the crowd. An appreciative chuckle rises from the circle of people around us.

"Whatever reason the lucky winner has for not coming forward yet," interjects Bran, rescuing me, "Jane and I are going to find them."

We are?

I shoot a quick, worried glance at Bran, but he's beaming at Molly and talking a bit more about how he'll use his investigative-reporter skills to figure out who won and how I'll be his research assistant.

I wish he'd talked with me about this first, but something about Bran's optimism and vulnerability in this moment makes my heart ache, and I remember him as a twelve-year-old nerd, checking out stacks of Hardy Boys and Nancy Drew books from the library. I can't not help him. Even if I'm the one he's looking for.

BRANDON KIM: Hi, everyone! Not sure if you caught the news tonight (lol, you were probably there, as it seemed like everyone in town was at the pumpkin patch this evening), but I'm trying to find the lucky lotto winner. I will be investigating over the next few days, but if anyone in town has any information, please reach out. It could be tips, clues, guesses—whatever you think will help! Here's my website information and my Instagram.

OLLIE WENTSER: So cool you're doing this, Bran!

MARY FULTON: It's weird though, right, that no one has come forward? Well, you know it's not me. Because if it were, I'd be on a jet to Bermuda already.

AMY PEMBERLY: It's super weird! I mean, how can it be so secret?

MARY FULTON: Maybe the person will come forward? I mean, I'm betting that someone will see the news segment and then check their ticket. Still believe that this is just a case of somebody getting too busy to check the numbers.

BRANDON KIM: That's a great point! It could all come out in the normal way over the next few days. But I'm definitely hoping to find the person so I can interview them.

J. WILKINS: I HAVE A TIP! The lucky ticket was sold at Wanda's. Why don't you talk to them?

BRANDON KIM: That's a great idea, and that's first on the list for my partner and me to check out tomorrow after school. Thanks!

CHAPTER SIX

SLAM MY LAPTOP CLOSED, DONE WITH INSTAGRAM AND FACEBOOK FOR the night. There are now over two hundred comments on the first thread about the winner, and Bran's thread is fast approaching that. If tonight has proven nothing else, it's that everyone in this damn town wants to know who won the lotto money.

How am I going to keep Bran off my trail? Would the clerk at Wanda's even remember me? They don't have a security system—they don't, right? I've never seen a camera there—but maybe I can keep Bran away from Wanda's? Though I know tomorrow he'll want to head there as soon as school's out. He already told the entire town that.

Running a hand over my face, I collapse onto my bed. I've been Googling the tragic stories of other lotto winners who've had terrible luck. I'm not sure why I keep looking these people up, but I can't seem to stop myself. Each one is more horrible than the last, and that's saying a lot since Abraham Shakespeare was buried under his patio. To keep them all together, I've been writing them in a notebook so I can remind myself of what not to do on the off chance I'm able to cash the ticket.

Flipping to an empty page in the notebook, I pick up the list

I started making, just so I can keep a handle on all the hot-mess things happening in my life right now:

JANE'S RIDICULOUS LIFE PROBLEMS:
You won the lotto. Shut up. It's not actually a problem, except . . .
   - You can't cash the ticket.
   - Because if you try to, the lotto commission will take away the money and charge you with a misdemeanor. All of which could be avoided by finding someone you trust to cash the ticket, except . . .
   - Mom is a train wreck of a human who will blow the money on absolute junk, and although being a lotto winner's kid might be okay, there's no guarantee I could get the money. I could ask Grandma, except . . .
   - She's a hippie who lives in a free-love commune (ahem, in a high-rise) and doesn't believe in possessions. Though maybe I'll try. I could ask Bran, except . . .
   - Oh, that's right, he's seventeen too. The only other person I know who's eighteen is Holden, and I could ask him, except . . .
   - He's an asshole. No exceptions.

I look at the list and add another problem:

   - Oh yeah, and Bran, my most beloved BFF, has decided that unmasking the lotto winner will help him get the internship he wants. Which would be fine, except . . .
   - I'm the winner, and I can't be unmasked until I figure all this out.
   - Which leaves me lying to my BFF on top of all this other stuff. And also leaves open the possibility that if I did somehow find someone to cash the ticket, and I become a millionaire, then my problems are really only just beginning because someone might kill me for the money, or even if not that, the rest of my life might be ruined because

"FORTUNA!" Mom's voice rings through the house. "Time to go!"

Ugh.

I just got home from the pumpkin farm half an hour ago, but Big Junk Dump day still awaits. After the interview, I helped Mrs. Kim in the snack bar for a few hours and then had to help Bran clean up the trash around the picnic area. When I got home, Mom's truck was in the driveway, and her door was closed. I'd hoped she'd gone to sleep, but no such luck.

Mom knocks on my door. I shove my notebook under my pillow and stand up.

"Hey," I say, opening the door. A yawn splits my face. "Any chance we can skip tonight? I'm super tired and have a long day at school tomorrow."

Mom twists her ponytail into a bun and then lets it fall. Her brow furrows, and she takes a deep breath, clearly warring with herself as she tries to figure out if she can choose me or the stuff. We've had this conversation before. If I don't help her pick up BJD junk, she'll keep bugging me all night as her anxiety ramps up about stuff being taken by the trash collectors early in the morning.

"I think we have to go now," says Mom quickly. "It won't be long. I promise. Please, Fortuna Jane?"

I sigh and nod. If we leave now, we could be done by one in the morning. Meaning I'll only get a few hours of sleep before school, but there's really no choice. "Let me get my shoes."

FIFTEEN MINUTES LATER, WE'RE CRUISING INTO TOWN. I'M DRIVING, and Mom has a flashlight pointed at the junk piles along the street. We pass one that's all old mattresses—thankfully, Mom doesn't want to start collecting those—and she also lets me pass the pile of tomato cages heaped among bags of yard waste.

We don't chitchat about our day or what's going on in our lives, and an anxious silence fills the truck cabin. For a moment, I imagine what it would be like to tell Mom about the winning ticket. I could do it right now. Just blurt it out. It's only five small words.

I practice saying them in my head. *"Mom, I won the lotto."*

Or, *"You're not going to believe this, Mom, but I won the lotto."*

Or, *"Mom, we'll never need to go through trash again, because we're now worth $58 million."*

That last one sounds wildly convincing, and it might just work. Maybe that huge sum would snap her out of this need to rescue other people's garbage? Maybe I could give it a try and then pass it off as a joke if it fails?

The words sit on my tongue, lumpy like mashed potatoes. I open my mouth, ready to—

"PULL OVER!" Mom shouts as we round a corner near the heart of our small downtown.

Uh-huh. Of course this made her stop.

I swallow, pushing any unsaid confessions back inside myself.

Heaped on the corner is a mountain of junk. It looks like the owners of the sprawling Victorian we've stopped in front of must be getting all new furniture, or maybe somebody died. Two recliners with stuffing poking out of them sit among a broken futon, boxes filled to the brim with photo frames, and much, much more. Mom's flashlight beam bounces all around the stuff, and she's out of the truck before I even stop beside the curb.

"Put down your light!" I whisper as the beam hits house windows. What we're doing is not technically illegal, but we've also had the police called on us before because we're out so late and making so much noise that we wake up somebody's kids or their dog.

Mom lowers her light, setting it on top of a dresser that's busted up and missing two of its drawers. "Can you believe all this stuff, Fortuna? Why would anyone throw it out?" She shoves a huge box toward me. "Go through that. Save anything of personal value!"

When she says it, it's both mission statement and a credo.

We Must Save Anything Someone Ever Loved!

There's an agitated desperation to her voice that's matched by her frenetic movements as she darts around the junk pile, pulling at stuffed animals, blankets, and books.

I take the box she's handed to me and rest it on the broken dresser beside her flashlight. Unlike Mom, who dives barehanded into junk finding, I always bring a pair of gardening gloves on BJD day. After slipping them onto my hands, I sift through the contents of the box.

It contains a few cheesy records ('80s BIG hair!), a stack of water-stained books, a bunch of hangers, some photo albums with no pictures in them, and then, inexplicably lumped at the bottom, is a wedding dress.

Weird.

I pull the dress out of the box. It unfolds like a satin and chiffon waterfall, with poufy sleeves bigger than my head. A wide brown stain (please let that be a coffee stain) covers the train of the dress.

"It's beautiful," Mom gasps. She drops the ugly lamp she was holding and runs one hand slowly along the tiny beads embroidered along the bodice. "Can you imagine throwing away a dress like this?"

I couldn't. But I also couldn't imagine keeping it. Or ever needing it, since I never plan on getting married. Still, though, I'm surprised the dress was so unceremoniously shoved among all the other junk in the box.

"I wonder what the story of it is," I say, half to myself.

Mom beams at me.

Shit. Wrong question.

"That's exactly what I've been trying to tell you!" Mom exclaims. "Stuff has stories, and someone certainly loved this once. How lucky that we found it!"

"Maybe they're getting rid of it because the marriage didn't work out or the bride died?"

As soon as the words are out, I clap a hand over my mouth, wishing I could shove them back inside. Mom collapses onto one of the broken armchairs, as if my words dropped her like an anvil. We don't talk about death. Or marriages that end in death. Or anything vaguely in the realm of any of that.

"I'm sorry," I say quietly. "I didn't mean—"

"It's nothing." Mom hops up and waves her hands in the air, as if she's clearing away a cloud of ghosts. "Don't just stand around. Let's get this stuff into the truck!"

I stay silent for a beat, giving her the space to say more if she wants. She doesn't, and I let out a long sigh. It's not that I want to get into our deepest feelings on the side of the road at midnight, but we probably should say all these unsaid things that have been building up for years between us. Someday, maybe we will. But not tonight.

"Which pieces do you want?" I ask.

Mom moves from box to box, then back to the armchair, then back to the dresser. "All of it! We'll go through it at home. Hurry, hurry. There's much more to be collected around town!"

Mom grabs the wedding gown from me, cradling it closely to

her chest. She lays it carefully on the front seat, where it sits like a ghostly bridal passenger. And just like that, I know she has a new mission: to save every wedding dress she comes across.

Shit.

With a long sigh, I push down any thoughts of my dad or who my mom was before he died, and I start loading boxes into the truck bed.

We make ten more stops before Mom's ready to go home. The wedding dress sits between us, and I pull my elbows in as I drive so I don't touch it. Along the way, Mom babbles about the lotto winner. I keep my mouth shut, letting her talk.

"And then I told Doris there was no way someone in our town has the ticket. Because if they did, they'd surely have come forward by now!" Mom lets out a giddy laugh, exhilarated by the night of rescuing things and the idea that the lotto winner could actually be someone in town.

Doris is the owner of Sammy's Storage Solutions (the place where Mom works) and Mom's best friend. Doris's husband was Sammy, a not-great guy who took off a few years ago with a twenty-two-year-old he met in a bar. When he left, Doris hired Mom full-time, which was both a good and bad thing. Doris shares Mom's passion for finding treasures in the trash, though she considers herself an expert on the level with the *Storage Wars* folks, so she only keeps items that she can sell.

The upside of their friendship is that Mom has someone in town who she can talk to besides me. The downside is that Doris lets Mom go through unclaimed or past-due storage lockers, which gives her a literal treasure trove. I wonder sometimes if they go around opening lockers during the day, just to see what's inside.

This is why I can't ask Mom to cash the ticket. She'd probably split the money with Doris, and they'd buy out all the storage lockers in the US or something. I'm so grateful I didn't say anything earlier.

Mom keeps talking until our house comes into view. We left the porch light on, and ghoulish shadows from all the discarded toys fill the yard. The back of the truck rides so low, it scrapes the ground as we pull into our gravel driveway. My arms ache from hauling things out of piles and lifting broken stuff into the truck. A wide yawn splits my face as I turn off the engine.

"Any chance we can unload this tomorrow?" The clock on the dashboard reads 1:30 a.m. I have to be up at six if I'm going to finish the math and English homework I didn't get to earlier.

Mom shakes her head, like I've suggested something utterly ridiculous. "You know the routine, Fortuna. We have to get it into the house."

"But there's no room in the house!" I burst out, my aching body and exhaustion bringing all my frustration to the surface.

"Nonsense," Mom says, carefully picking up the wedding dress. She opens the passenger-side door. "We have loads of space. In fact, I've been thinking about it: Your room could always use a bit more stuff."

"Absolutely not."

She shoots me a calculating look, like she's trying to figure out what she'd have to say to me to get me to relent. But I'm not budging on this point.

"If you put any of this crap in my room," I say firmly, "I'm moving in with Grandma."

Mom laughs then. "She doesn't have room for you in that tiny apartment!" Her voice is almost gleeful. "But don't worry, you'll be off to college soon enough."

"I literally cannot wait," I mutter under my breath.

If I can find someone other than Mom to cash my $58 million secret for me, then maybe I could get out of here sooner. *But if I did that,* whispers some part of me, *then who would help Mom? Or remind her to eat?*

With a weary sigh, I untie the ropes holding the stuff in place in the back of the truck and start unloading.

I FALL INTO BED AT TWO THIRTY IN THE MORNING, FEELING LIKE I've run wind sprints or played back-to-back soccer games. I did, at least, change out of my filthy clothes, but facing a shower was too much. Hating myself a little for skipping brushing my teeth, I check that the lotto ticket is still in its place—it is, thank God.

With clumsy fingers, I set my phone alarm for six. At least I'll get a few hours of sleep.

When my head hits the pillow, something rustles underneath it. Has Mom shoved something in here? Personalized stationery or a stack of unused wedding invitations? I swear, if those are under my pillow—or if she's been in my room—I'm moving out tomorrow.

Fumbling in the dark, I flick on my phone's light and reach under my pillow. Oh. Right. Not Mom's stuff, but my notebook with the lotto-winner stories and my list of problems.

As tired as I am, I can't help but read the list again and skim the stories on the top page. Talk about stuff to give me bad dreams.

THE BIG BOOK OF LOTTO WINNER FAILS
Paraphrased from news sources and collected for posterity
by Jane Belleweather

UNLUCKY LOTTO WINNER NUMBER TWO:

Jeffrey Dampier is another example of someone who won the lotto and lost everything. His prize for winning the Illinois Lottery was $20 million, and he shared it with his family.

But, as these things go, somebody got greedy. A few years after he won the jackpot, Dampier's sister-in-law and her boyfriend kidnapped him and shot him in the back of the head. The couple is now in prison for life, and Dampier is just another example of what a windfall with so many zeroes after it can do to people.

Note to self: This is example number two of a lotto winner being murdered by family or loved ones for the sake of the prize. A disturbing trend, to say the least.

UNLUCKY LOTTO WINNER NUMBER THREE:

Example number three isn't quite so grim, but what a mess. Evelyn Adams from New Jersey somehow won the lottery in both 1985 ($3.9 million) and 1986 ($1.4 million). As one does, she gave away some of the money to friends and then the rest of it went to feed her gambling habit. By 2000, she was broke and living in a trailer park.

Note to self: This quote from Evelyn gives me chills: "Winning the lottery isn't always what it's cracked up to be. Everybody wanted my money. Everybody had their hand out."

UGHHHHHHHH.

CHAPTER SEVEN

M Y ALARM GOES OFF ON FRIDAY MORNING AT SIX, AND I WANT TO fling my phone into the sun. But I shut it off and get up. First a shower, then homework, and then I'll somehow drag myself through the day.

I take *Sea Change* off the shelf and check it again. The ticket is still there, wedged at the beginning of "Beyond Flotsam and Jetsam," the chapter about the devastating effect of plastics on the ocean. I hold it in my hand for a moment. It's still unsigned. But I can't sign it now because that's acknowledging that I bought it as a minor. Which means no one would get the prize.

As I hold the ticket, I wonder: Is it a ticket to freedom and the independent life I want, or something that will leave me chained to a lifetime of people bugging me about money? Is it even possible to actually cash it? Can I find someone over eighteen who will cash it for me and give me the money—well, I guess they'd probably want to share it—or is there some way I can make it seem like I actually was eighteen when I bought it?

I still don't know. All I'm certain of is that for now, the best bet is to leave the ticket unsigned and in my room. I put it back, determined to do more research later today, and head into the shower.

Mom's still snoring in her room when I creep out of mine. It's hardly fair that the adult in the house gets to sleep in and doesn't have to report for duty in the real world until ten. Because I love her underneath it all, I leave her a cup of coffee covered with a saucer. Because I'm still mad at her for dragging me along on BJD night, I don't leave a note.

One reason I'm up so early—besides needing to scrub last night's Big Junk Dump adventure off my skin and get my homework done in the school library—is for the quiet space of a walk to school. It's more than two miles, but I can't face the bus and I don't want to ask Bran to pick me up. And extricating my bike from the stuff Mom piled on it last night would just make more noise.

Better to walk alone down a country road as morning breaks and pray no semis come barreling around a corner and flatten me.

The sky lightens in the east, a peach soft glow, like a zillion grandmas just turned on pastel-shaded reading lamps. On either side of me, tall rows of corn rise. This late in October, the cornstalks are brown and rattle like skeleton fingers in the morning breeze. A flock of Canadian geese fly across the horizon, soaring in a V formation and filling the air with honks.

It's beautiful. Truly. I tilt my head back, taking in the morning air. It smells like earth, the changing seasons, and a hint of winter. It smells like home.

But—as an overpowering whiff of cow manure and something most foul from the enormous chicken farms a few miles away hits me—my fond feelings wane. I'm confident I could get used to a new home either on or near the ocean. Like, immediately.

Before I can think much more about that, a car whips around the corner. Its music is blaring and its headlights are on. It's still too dark to see who's behind the wheel, and they probably don't see me, but I'm taking no chances. I jump off the side of the road, landing in a shallow ditch. My heart pounds.

I've read news stories about situations like this. Girls get picked up in the early hours of the morning by strangers and are never seen again. At least not until their bodies are found outside of Vegas or something.

The car roars past me, and I'm clambering out of the ditch when it stops and then backs up.

Shit.

There's literally no one else on this road with me. I pull out my phone, taking a picture of the car and the license plate.

Blue Honda Civic, WI tags.

Feeling just a touch dramatic, I send Bran a text and the picture of the car:

It's 6:45 a.m. and I'm on the road into town. This car is stopping. If you don't see me at school, you know who has killed me. Avenge me.

All joking aside, my pulse pounds as the driver's-side window of the Civic rolls down and the music stops. I step back, far enough away so the driver can't grab me. I can't see them through the tinted front window.

"Jane?" a familiar voice calls.

I step up to the window. Sure enough, it's Holden. Goddammit.

"What are you doing out here? You scared me to death and nearly killed me!"

"Sorry about that," Holden says with a rueful smile. "Didn't expect to see anyone out this way so early."

"Did you get a new car?"

When we were dating, he still drove his dad's old truck. He raises his sunglasses, and his blue eyes catch some of the morning light.

"Senior-year present to myself. It's not a Ferrari—yet. Wait until I make my first million."

Holden laughs confidently, like he's absolutely certain the universe will let him make those millions. I guess it wouldn't be fair to say he totally changed after his ridiculous *Wolf of Wall Street* camp. He always did want a Ferrari, for example. But he was also still the guy who'd wade into creeks with me and pick up trash for Ecology Club. These days, I have no idea if any part of that guy is left.

I give a weak laugh along with him. "How'd you get the car?"

"I've been investing my savings for a few years now, and some of it really paid off. I had enough to get this car and still keep a bunch of money in my funds."

"That's great," I say. Two days ago, I couldn't ever imagine having enough money to buy a car, but I guess I could do that now. If I can get this ticket cashed. "Where are you going this morning?"

Holden smiles at me. That stupid half smile that makes my insides melt. "To get coffee at Starbucks. What are you doing out here?"

"Trying to get run over by fools who drive too fast."

Holden snorts. "Want to get coffee with me?"

I kind of really do. But that would mean spending time with Holden, which is something I've been firmly avoiding since the breakup.

I hold up my travel mug. "I'm covered. See you at school." I start walking toward town.

"Hey, Jane, wait!" Holden calls out. He's out of his car and striding toward me. "Let me at least give you a ride to school. You're going to get run over out here, for real."

He looks like he wants to say more, but that's a privilege he lost when he dumped me.

"I'm fine," I say, waving a hand dismissively.

"C'mon. For old time's sake. Plus, we can go over our plan for the Ecology Club field trip today."

I stop walking and spin around. "What are you talking about?"

Holden flashes that smirky-smoldery smile of his, and I want to dump my travel mug of coffee on him. "You forgot, didn't you?"

"I didn't."

I totally did. Despite the fact that Mrs. Davis reminded me about it before yesterday's Ecology Club meeting. But now I remember. With all my worrying about the lotto ticket plus work last night, and then my exhaustion from BJD day, I completely spaced on the fact that the Ecology Club is taking a class of third graders on a field trip to the Aquarium Oasis fish store in Madison today. We'd gotten the whole day off classes after first period and everything. I'd also forgotten that Holden and I are the high-school guides. Me because the field trip had been my idea, and Holden because his sister is part of the third-grade class we're taking.

"Fine," I say, stomping back to his car. "You can give me a ride to school."

"Thank you for allowing me this honor," he says, making a small bow. "But first, I'm buying you a Starbucks drink. I know it's better than that swill your mom keeps at home."

He's not wrong, and as I slip into the passenger seat, I have to smile a bit. Fine. Okay. Holden is still a little bit charming.

CHAPTER EIGHT

Bran texts me once we're headed back from the Starbucks in the next town over.

BRAN: JANE! Are you dead? Reply before I call in the National Guard.

JANE: lol. I'm fine. Sorry to panic you. It was actually Holden in the car this morning. We got coffee.

BRAN: . . . Jane. No. Tell me you didn't hang out with him.

JANE: It's fine. I swear. See you in class.

Bran tries to corner me in first period, but I just hand him a Starbucks chai (bought by me, not Holden) and flash him a smile as I plop into the desk in front of his.

Our English teacher starts in about Shakespeare, and Bran sends a note onto my desk. I unfold the small square of paper.

DON'T YOU DARE EVEN THINK ABOUT FALLING FOR HOLDEN AGAIN.

I roll my eyes and take a sip of my vanilla latte. I throw the note back with a quick: Don't worry, he's still the worst.

Bran's reply is quick: Fine. But if you start to not hate him again, text me. I'll remind you why he's awful.

But is he really?

Yes. Of course he is. But that doesn't mean I haven't missed him just a little bit. And this morning, laughing with him in his car, it felt almost like normal again.

Clearly being a possible millionaire-in-the-making is messing with my judgment. I spend the rest of English class remembering all the things I hate about Holden.

HATING HOLDEN IS WHAT'S STILL ON MY MIND AS WE DRIVE TO THE Aquarium Oasis. I was going to ride the bus with the third graders, but Holden offered me a ride, and I have to admit his company was decidedly more appealing than a bus full of thirty screaming eight-year-olds.

Still, even as he's popping on a playlist we used to listen to, I remind myself of how awful he is: He doesn't like dogs or cats; he swears the classics are the best things ever written and will only read a book written after 1960 if it's been assigned; his commitment to environmental issues is dicey at best, since he drinks out of one-off water bottles; and he never read the copy of *Sea Change* I gifted him a week after we first kissed.

But some small voice also asks: Is all that stuff really so bad?

I'm not sure, and another voice reminds me of what he has going for him, or what he *had* going for him, before the breakup: Besides the perfect, shiny, rom-com life I thought we were living, Holden also used to come pick me up every morning so I didn't have to walk to school; he listened to me bitch about my mom without saying anything; he took me out on his family's boat and then was okay when I just wanted to float on the water, not talking. We learned so much about sex and our bodies together.

Dammit.

The internal war rages inside me as we pull onto the highway, and I shut my eyes, hoping sleep will drag me under so I don't have to talk to Holden.

"So, what do you think of this lotto-winner news?" asks Holden. "Man, I wish I'd bought a ticket. If I'd won, I'd be out of this town and off to spend my millions in, like, a heartbeat."

My dreamy clouds of almost-sleep disappear. "What?" I say, sitting up abruptly. I give a big fake yawn to cover up the panicky note in my voice. "Sorry, I didn't go to bed until late last night."

"Big Junk Dump day?" Holden raises an eyebrow, and I hate him for knowing why that would mean anything to me.

"Uh-huh." That's all I'm giving him.

"I can let you rest," he says.

"Why are you being so nice?" I blurt out. Obviously, the question has been on my mind all morning.

"Because we're friends," says Holden, as if that sums it all up.

"Are we?"

"Yes."

"You broke up with me, remember?"

"Well, yeah . . ."

"We dated for two years, and we broke up out of the blue because you said you were unhappy and weren't into me anymore . . ."

This is a lot of anger and unsaid things that I'm throwing at him, but I don't want to talk about the lotto winner. And I would love an explanation. Or at least more than the "I don't think we're a good fit as a couple anymore" and the other generic reasons he offered when he ended our relationship.

Holden rubs one hand along the back of his neck and has the good grace to look embarrassed. He also looks super hot as he drives one-handed. I hate my stupid lizard brain for noticing that.

"I'm sorry," he says slowly. "Breaking it off like that was a bad idea on my part."

Wait. Did he just say that?

"It really hurt me," I admit. And then I don't say what I really want to say: Was it such a bad idea that he's thinking we should get back together? Is that something he's even interested in?

Because I'm not sure how I feel about that. Being this close to Holden, and being honest with him, really feels like I'm on a tightrope walking over a shark tank.

"I'm sorry I hurt you," he says. And he sounds like he really is. Or maybe I'm just too tired to tell the difference. "I really miss you, Jane. Like, nothing is as fun without you around."

Well. I've been called a lot of things, but super fun is not one of them.

And that's when I realize I've missed him too.

"Oh shut up," I say with a long sigh. "Let's not do this now. Tell me about your birthday. What else did you get, besides this car?"

Holden glances over at me quickly, as if he wants to say more.

"And keep your eyes on the road. We have third graders to chaperone. We must arrive in one piece."

"Yes, ma'am," Holden says with that easy, friendly laugh of his. He sounds like his old self.

God. Have I actually missed his laugh? I should text Bran right now, tell him I'm in danger, but Holden's talking about how his family went to Hawaii over fall break, how he celebrated his eighteenth birthday on the beach, and how he thought of me the entire time they were at the whale sanctuary.

"Wait, wait, wait," I say, rewinding his last sentences. "Say that again. You actually went to the Humpback Whale National Marine Sanctuary?"

Holden laughs again. "Yes. I've been trying to tell you about it since we got back, but you wouldn't talk to me. I got you something. Look in the glove box."

"I still hate you," I say under my breath as I open the glove box.

There's a blue paper bag inside with a humpback whale stamped on it. I open it, pulling out a small enamel pin. On it is a picture of a humpback whale breaching beside a boat.

"It's perfect," I admit grudgingly, as I pin it to my backpack.

"We went out on a boat just like the one on the pin," says Holden. "I got seasick, but the whales were magnificent."

"Now I really hate you." But I can't keep the smile out of my voice. "The only way you can make up for it is to tell me absolutely everything about the visit."

Holden smiles. "Deal."

We spend the rest of the ride talking about what Holden saw, how it felt to be so close to the whales, and my plans for being an oceanographer.

"Enjoy the sea sickness," he says. "I still love nature, but I'm keeping my feet planted firmly on the ground. The deeper in the woods, the better."

"I'm ocean and you're woods. This is why we didn't work," I say, but all my bite is gone. In fact, I find myself smiling at Holden as we pull into the parking lot of the aquarium store.

Where is Bran when I need him to whack me over the head with a fedora?

"Let's ride back together," Holden suggests. "I'm sure we still have lots more to talk about."

Before I can disagree or say anything at all, a bunch of third graders start pouring out of the bus. We get out of the car and wave to them.

"Hi, Holden!" shouts Holden's sister, Harper, tumbling down the bus stairs. She's still tan from their fall-break trip, and her long hair is in two pigtails. She flings her arms around her brother. "You made it!"

"Of course I did," he says with a smile. Harper hangs on to the hug a second longer, and Holden shrugs at me over her head. I always liked how good he was with kids.

"Hi, Harper," I say when she lets go.

She gives me a quick look and then smiles. It's like the sun hitting the ocean. "JANE!" she squeals and hugs me too. "It's so good to see you."

I spent so much time with Harper over the last few years, it was a bit like she was my little sister as well. As I hug her, I can't help the smile that creeps onto my face.

THE AQUARIUM OASIS GLOWS BLUE LIKE THE INSIDE OF A FAIRY GROTTO, and the entire place is filled with quiet, steady bubbling noises from hundreds of fish tanks. Peace fills me as I step inside. Some people have churches, but I need watery spaces.

"Ooooohhhh," all the third graders say in unison as we step inside. Their teacher and some of the parent guides usher them toward the largest tank in the store.

"It looks like a rave," whispers Holden, standing next to me in front of the group.

"Shut up," I whisper, but it comes out almost playful. He grins at me.

"Why is it so blue?" one kid asks from the back of the group.

"This is called actinic light," I say to the third graders. "It's what coral needs to grow when they're not in the ocean."

"How many of you have seen the ocean?" Holden asks smoothly. Most of the kids hold up their hands, but a few don't.

"Well," Holden continues, "I bet a lot of you haven't seen coral in the ocean, right?"

The kids who didn't have their hands up look a little less awkward.

"I HAVE!" Harper calls out.

"You have," says Holden. "We went snorkeling over fall break, and it was awesome. But even if you haven't seen the ocean, how many of you have seen *Finding Nemo?*"

Every hand in the room goes up. Holden nudges me. Right, oceanographer go time.

"So, imagine you're a coral in the ocean," I say. "You're not hanging out in the school cafeteria, underneath those bright fluorescent lights, are you?"

All the kids shake their heads.

"That's right," I continue. "All the light you're getting is filtered through layers of water. That's what the folks here are trying to do. This blue light helps the corals grow and thrive. It tricks them into thinking they're deep in the ocean."

Just like me, I think. *This blue light is what I need to grow and thrive.*

I tell them a few more facts about the ocean and then let them loose.

"Don't touch anything," Holden reminds them. "Even in the open tanks. This isn't a place for touching, like the aquarium in Milwaukee."

Harper pulls her hand back right before it hits an open tank of coral. I smile at Holden and we split up, moving among the groups of kids and the parent volunteers who are with them.

I stop in front of a tank full of rare fish.

"These all came from Australia," I tell the kids.

"Just like Nemo!" one shouts.

"Exactly," I say. "These fish have had a long journey."

"I bet they miss their parents," says Harper, staring at a pair of yellow fish as they drift past.

"They're probably happy where they are," says Holden, coming up to our group.

There's a light pressure on my hand, and then his fingers curl around mine for a moment. Without thinking, I wrap my fingers around his. I must be losing it. I've been lured into complacency by the blue lights and the soothing bubbles of all the aquarium pumps.

Without a word, I drop Holden's hand and walk over to a nearby group of kids.

I TAKE THE BUS BACK HOME. TO BLOCK OUT THE LOUD CHATTER OF THE kids, I pop my headphones in and look at my phone. The article about lotto winners who lost it all is still pulled up, and I find myself reading, no music turned on, unable to look away. As the bus rattles along the highway, I fill my notebook with more stories of unlucky winners, which just barely takes my mind off of Holden, and how unusually nice he's being, and what he might have meant by being sorry we broke up.

THE BIG BOOK OF LOTTO WINNER FAILS, CONTINUED
Paraphrased from news sources and collected for posterity
by Jane Belleweather

UNLUCKY LOTTO WINNER NUMBER FOUR: THE CASE OF UROOJ KHAN

This one is particularly macabre. Forty-six-year-old Urooj Khan won only $1 million on a scratch-off ticket. (That's fifty-eight times less than what I've won, which means I now think of $1 million as not very much, which is so messed up.)

The day after he won, Urooj dropped dead. Who was to blame? Was it a heart attack? Something more sinister? Suspicion and disbelief tore his family apart, and years later, a blood test revealed deadly levels of cyanide in his blood. No one was ever charged, but his sister-in-law and her father were suspected. Somehow, the family moved on, and his winnings were split. But his family (and the Chicago police) still wonder to this day who killed him.

Note to self: Although this case is shrouded in mystery, and correlation is not causation, it's pretty clear by now that winning lots of money makes people do terrible things. Like, load up a dinner with poison and serve it with a smile.

UNLUCKY LOTTO WINNER NUMBER FIVE: JACK WHITTAKER, AN OBJECT LESSON

Jack Whittaker is harder to feel sorry for than Urooj Khan, because this lucky bastard was already rich (worth something like $17 million) and then he won another $315 million in Powerball. (THREE HUNDRED AND FIFTEEN MILLION! I can't even imagine!)

Jack did some good with the money, like donating to charities and setting up foundations, but he also seemingly couldn't get enough of strip clubs. Get this: The guy got robbed more than once outside of strip clubs, and each time the thieves took hundreds of thousands of dollars from his car.

(Get an effing bank account already, Jack. Sheesh.)

But that's not the worst part: Jack became an alcoholic, he and his wife divorced, and his granddaughter (whom Jack was supplying with thousands of dollars every month) died of a drug overdose.

Whittaker and his wife both said they wished he had torn up the ticket.

NOTE TO SELF: JACK WON NEARLY A HUNDRED TIMES MORE THAN I DID AND BROUGHT MISERY TO EVERYONE HE LOVED.

MY FOLLOW-UP QUESTIONS:

Do I tear up the ticket???

Or am I the most entitled, shitty human alive for not finding a way to cash it and try to do some good????

Also, Holden is eighteen now and not being a total jackass. Is he even an option for cashing the ticket? Would he give me the money?

(No, Jane. Stop. Don't even consider this. Bad idea.)

CHAPTER NINE

"WHAT DO YOU MEAN YOU HELD HANDS WITH HOLDEN?" BRAN asks, nearly spitting out the mouthful of chips he's just stuffed into his face.

We're crammed inside the Kim family pumpkin farm's ticket booth, sitting behind the low counter. Bran is eating from a supersized bag of chips he's pulled out of his backpack. For scale: There's barely room for the two of us, the backpack, and the bag of chips inside the tiny booth. But this was the only place we could chat without Bran's mom assigning us separate tasks.

"It wasn't a big deal," I say quietly, so the line of people outside of the booth doesn't hear us.

"Of course it's a big deal. We hate him," Bran mutters. He offers me the bag of chips. I shake my head.

"I know we hate him," I say, running a hand over my super-short hair and then fiddling with the row of earrings in my right ear. When did I become such a fidgeter? "But he was nice today."

"He's not nice! Remember how he'd do stuff like make you think things were your fault when they weren't? Like that time when we were at the carnival last year, and you both were in the seat below Sofie and me. Remember what happened to his phone when he was trying to take a picture of you two? Sofie and I saw that *he* dropped it, but he blamed you for breaking it for the rest of the night. Or what about the way he was always saying you made him late for movies and stuff, even though he was the one who could never decide what he wanted at the snack bar? Or the way he made you second-guess what you wanted? C'mon, Jane. He was a jerk."

Those are all true statements, and they are certainly not part of the easy, breezy rom-com relationship I thought I had. But there's a chance we're remembering things wrong.

"Maybe he was just really stressed out? Maybe his family was going through some stuff?"

"Jane. No. We don't feel sorry for Holden. That's a rule."

"Fine," I say, smiling at a small girl in a witch costume who's standing beside her parents in line. "But what if he's changed?"

"Who cares?! He's a douchebag, and you deserve someone better!"

The little girl in the witch costume widens her eyes, and her mother glares at us.

"Sorry," I mutter, handing them their tickets to the hayride.

I turn back to Bran. "So, how is Sofie? I saw her Instagram photos from yesterday. She's so lucky to live in Sydney. Can you even—"

"Jane, don't change the subject. You don't need Holden in your life."

With a long sigh, I slump into the chair behind the counter. "Fine. You're right."

"He wants something," says Bran. "Trust me. I can just tell."

"With what? Your investigative instincts?"

He makes a face at me. "Yes, those. Don't let yourself get drawn back into his orbit."

He's right, of course. Holden's orbit is planetary. It loops around and around, and before you know it, he's the center of everything else in your life. Because he shows up with coffee out of the blue and takes you on surprise trips to places you think you'd hate, like waterparks, and then convinces you to love them like he does.

I squeeze some hand sanitizer into my palm, as if that would cleanse me of the feeling of Holden's hand in mine.

"Mandatory subject change: Tell me about the investigation," I say. "I'm sorry I didn't get to help with anything after school."

I had rushed straight from the Aquarium Oasis field trip to soccer practice and then just barely made it to work at five, in my sweaty practice clothes. Bran had a bowl of his mom's noodle soup waiting for me in the ticket booth, which I slurped down in about ten seconds.

"We're not done with this Holden conversation," warns Bran. "But, okay. Subject change noted. The investigation is not going at all."

"Did you go by Wanda's?"

Bran nods. "I did, but it's closed."

"Closed? They're never closed."

"Except when they sell a winning lotto ticket and get a fifty thousand dollar payout for being the ones who sold it."

My stomach sinks. "Doesn't the winner have to come forward before they get that?"

Bran shakes his head. "Nope. I looked it up. They get the payout immediately, and in Wanda's case, she left a sign on the door saying she and Mary Anne are on vacation for the first time in ten years."

Welp. At least somebody is enjoying their surprise riches. I just hope they don't end up having to give them back (or worse) if the world finds out they sold the ticket to me as a minor. Knowing

Wanda and her family's happiness is at stake unless I figure out what to do with this ticket just makes finding someone to cash it ASAP that much more urgent.

But who?

Mom? Grandma? Holden? Is there no one else I can trust?

There really isn't. And I will have to choose from these three soon.

Ugh.

AMY PEMBERLY: Starting a new thread here about the lotto winner because I seriously cannot believe no one has come forward.

MARY FULTON: Same! How can you just be sitting on all that money? Like, if you don't want it, give it to someone who does!

LISA HAWKINS: Agreed! It's unthinkable. Send some of that money my way. Lord knows I could use it for bills or gas in my car.

AMY PEMBERLY: I think it's a sin to waste all that money and not come forward.

MARY FULTON: They have 180 days to claim it; we could be in for a long wait, folks.

J. WILKINS: They're a coward for not coming forward.

MARY FULTON: Now, don't be so harsh. Maybe they've got something going on we don't know about.

J. WILKINS: YEAH right. Like they're now worth more than the entire budget of this town for the year. Talk to me later about all their problems. [100 more comments]

CHAPTER TEN

D ID YOU KNOW MOST OF THE OCEAN IS A WATERY DESERT? IT'S HUGE and empty, with predators cruising endlessly. At least that's what David Attenborough reports in his series for the BBC, *The Blue Planet*.

I'm deep in a *The Blue Planet* marathon on Saturday morning, and I'm alternating between jotting down facts about the ocean in my notebook, avoiding Bran's phone calls, composing replies that I then delete to Holden's friendly text—*It was fun to hang out! We should do it again soon*—and doing homework. I've seen all the *The Blue Planet* episodes a dozen times already, but Attenborough's soothing voice and the magnificent, aloof, turbulent ocean are the only company I can handle right now.

The Facebook threads about the lotto winner are getting worse. I don't normally go on Facebook, but now I can't seem to stay out of the town's group. It's like watching an accident in slow motion. People seem genuinely pissed that no one has come forward, and there's been talk of bodily harm. As I read through the threads, all I can think about are those predators in the deep, empty places of the ocean, cruising around, looking for something to sink their teeth into.

Fifty-eight million dollars is a lot to sink your teeth into.

At three o'clock in the afternoon, there's a knock on my window. Although my room is on the second story of the farmhouse, and that should be a deterrent to using the window as a door, I immediately know it's Bran. Because who else would show up at my house like this? I also know he'll keep knocking unless I answer.

I somehow manage to haul myself off my bed and push the curtains aside. Then I nearly fall over.

Eeeek.

It's not Bran. It's Holden. He's balancing on the top of a rickety metal pool ladder (one of Mom's oldest finds) and holding two cups of Starbucks.

"Uhm . . . hi," I say as I open the window. I try not to cringe as I imagine how Holden must be seeing me: braless, wearing a tank top and leggings and no makeup, which could be an effortlessly chic look on some girls, but not me.

"Brought you coffee," says Holden by way of greeting. He hands up both of our cups. "It's a vanilla latte. Can I come in?"

Something in my heart lurches. Holden never used the front door when we were dating because I didn't want him to see the overall state of the house. This is a few steps too close to those old times.

"Why?" I can't keep the note of suspicion from my voice. After my talk with Bran yesterday, and about a thousand pep talks with myself today, I vowed to keep my distance from Holden.

"Because I can hear David Attenborough's voice from out here, and no one has seen you all day. That can mean only one thing: *The Blue Planet* binge. Which in turn can only mean one thing: that you're super stressed or worried about something and need some company."

I hate that he knows this about me.

"What if I don't want company?"

Holden shrugs. "Then I'll leave the coffee and be on my way."

I sigh. I do want company. Because being alone with my enormous $58 million secret, my homework, and Mom's piles of junk cannot be good for any seventeen-year-old.

"Fine."

He grins. Then, in one fluid movement, he hoists himself into my room. His presence fills it.

"I like what you did with the place," he says, gesturing to the pile of papers on the bed. "And I still haven't read this book. Even though you gave me a copy ages ago."

He picks up *Sea Change* and turns it over to read the back-cover copy. Putting our cups down so fast some of the coffee sloshes onto my nightstand, I snatch the book from Holden's hands. The winning lotto ticket is still inside, and I've only looked at it like nine hundred times today. All Holden would have to do is flip through the pages, and the truth would be out.

Of course, if I just told him about it and asked him to cash the ticket for me, then problem solved. But can I really trust Holden to give me the money? What if he took all the money for himself and went off to live that super-rich lifestyle he's always talking about?

"This book is not that great," I lie, shoving *Sea Change* into my backpack, along with all the bio homework on my bed. Which leaves the bed very open. Which leaves me very open to remembering the last time Holden was here. When we were having sex. In my bed. A few hours before he broke up with me.

Holden shoots me a look, as if he's remembering the same thing. He bites his lower lip but doesn't say anything. "So are you going to the lake tonight?"

This is a Saturday-night tradition in Lakesboro. Every night until the snow comes, a bunch of high-school kids take over the beach for bonfires, drinking, and hanging out on the lake. Most of the kids in town have boats, including Holden. Since I don't even have a kayak, being on Holden's boat is one of my only chances to be out there. And my soul could desperately use some on-the-water time right now.

But this is Holden.

Nothing is ever simple with him, and although it hurts me physically to say it, I stay strong. "Not tonight. I'm staying home to catch up on some schoolwork."

"C'mon, Jane. Forget homework and come to the lake with me. It'll be fun," Holden persists, with a look that's more promise than anything else. He steps forward, and our bodies are now inches apart. His face is so close, I can count all the freckles his trip to Hawaii has brought out across his nose. He smells like sunshine and his shampoo. The combination makes my insides ache. My traitorous breath catches in my treacherous throat.

There's another knock on my window, and then Bran's face appears. "Jane? What the shit? I've been calling you all . . ." His voice trails off when he sees Holden standing so close to me.

"Hey, Bran," I say, stepping away from Holden like he's on fire. I stride toward the window. "Uhm, come on in."

Bran scowls and then heaves himself through my window too. His trench coat—yes, he's wearing a vintage tan trench coat along with a T-shirt and his gray fedora—catches on the windowsill, and he tugs at it. When it comes free, he tumbles into the room in a tangle of limbs. Brushing himself off, Bran stands up quickly.

And there we all are.

Me, Holden, and Bran, just casually standing in my bedroom.

Inches away from my basket of dirty laundry—which naturally, with my luck, has a pair of bright-red underwear on top—and my backpack, which holds the book that holds the $58 million lotto ticket.

Not awkward at all. Nope.

HA!

"What's he doing here?" Bran shoots Holden a poisonous look.

"He brought coffee," I say in the world's most pathetic attempt to find some social footing. I hold up my latte. "Want a sip?"

"I'm hoping to take Jane to the lake tonight," Holden says smoothly. "What are *you* doing here?"

Bran turns to me, eyes wide. "I'm her best friend. I don't need a reason to be here. You're not going to the lake with *him*, are you?"

I glare at Bran, annoyed suddenly by his protectiveness. "I'm not sure. He just got here, and I'm undecided on my evening's activities."

"Come with me to the Harvest Festival," says Bran. "I've got a lead on the lotto ticket, and I want to ask some questions."

I should definitely tag along with Bran so I can throw him off the scent if he gets too close to my secret.

Holden shoots us a look that makes it clear that attending the Harvest Festival is the dorkiest way imaginable to spend a Saturday night. He slings an arm over my shoulder. "Choose the lake, Jane. Have some fun."

"I'm going with Bran," I say, shrugging off Holden's arm. I take a step away before my poor, confused body can be swarmed with more hormones.

"Plus—as we've already covered—I'm her best friend," adds Bran. "And you're just the dick who broke her heart."

Holden has the good grace to blush. "Okay, okay. I can take a hint. I'll see you around, Jane." He starts toward the window.

"Wait!" I call, following him to the windowsill. My hand rests on his shoulder for a moment, sending a thrill of heat through me. I drop it faster than I would a jellyfish. "Thanks for the coffee. I'll try to get to the lake later, after the festival."

Holden smiles at me again, and my insides melt. "I'll count on it. Text me."

Then he's gone, and I'm left with a furious Bran.

"Don't even try to explain," says Bran, jamming his fedora down to his eyebrows. "If you want to hang out with Holden, that's your business. Just be careful."

"I'm not even sure what's happening there," I admit. "He just sort of showed up."

"Do you still like him?"

I shrug. "It's complicated. Maybe he just reminds me of a time when I was happy? Or he's a distraction? Or maybe he's my great love, like in the movies."

Bran snorts. "He's not your great love. I refuse to accept that, because it means I'll have to hang out with him for the rest of our lives. But if you want to go out on the lake with him tonight, I won't tie you up and lock you in my trunk."

"Super generous of you. Now, what's your plan?"

Bran clearly has more to say about Holden, but he plops into my desk chair and pulls a list of questions from his pocket. "I need to go through the festival crowd tonight asking these questions."

I take the list from him, reading out loud in as dramatic a voice as I can muster to dispel some of the tension in the room.

Have you ever played the lottery?

Where were you the night the lotto ticket was purchased?

Did you go to Wanda's that night? If yes, then what time were you there?

If you aren't the winner, do you have any clue who it might be?

What would you do with the money if you had won it?

"I don't see how the last one is relevant," I say, reading over the list again. The lotto ticket is inches away from Bran. All he would have to do is lean over, unzip my bag, pull out the book, and mystery solved.

It's possible he could even help me figure out whom I should ask to cash it. But that's a lot to put on him. I promise myself that I'll tell him soon.

"I'm hoping to start a conversation with these questions," Bran says as he takes the list back. "I want to get people talking, and I'm hoping they reveal some useful information. Can you help?"

He looks at me expectantly, and I let out a long breath. "Of course I'll help."

"Even if it takes all night?"

"Even if it takes all night."

Bran grins at me. "That's what I like to hear. Congratulations, you've earned this." He reaches into his coat pocket and pulls out a slightly smashed fedora that's identical to his, except it's light blue with a pink band.

"You can't be serious." I hold the fedora at arms length. It looks like something a Muppet would wear.

"Deadly serious," says Bran.

He laughs then, and I shove the fedora onto my head. If I can't tell Bran the truth, at least I can make him laugh.

CHAPTER ELEVEN

THE HARVEST FESTIVAL IS REALLY HOPPING BY THE TIME WE GET there. It's overcast, and a chilly breeze shakes orange and red leaves from the trees. But despite the cool temperature and the threat of storm clouds on the horizon, people fill the center of town. Dozens of tents selling whimsically painted pumpkins, wooden *Welcome* signs that have somehow taken over every doorstep in town, and lots of unusual crafts line Main Street. Pots of yellow and red mums surround the bandstand in the middle of town, and dozens of enormous pumpkins ("All from our farm," Bran tells me proudly) are scattered around the square.

Kids laugh and chatter by the children's area, where there are toffee apples, face painting, and a costume contest.

"Where do we start?" I ask, scanning the crowd. I take a long sip of the coffee Holden brought me and try not to think about how much nicer it would be out on the quiet lake with him, rather than surrounded by surging crowds.

It looks like nearly everyone in Lakesboro is here, along with a bunch of people from out of town too. Cars parked around the square have license plates from several different states. Clumps of preteens stand around, laughing and joking; families with little kids spill into the green space in the middle of downtown; and lots of older people—probably long-term residents of the town—amble slowly around the square, shopping, eating, and greeting one another.

Bran checks his watch. "We have an hour until the music at the bandstand starts, so let's split up. You go that way, I'll take this way, and we'll meet in the middle. Then we can regroup if the questions aren't working."

Shit. Splitting up wasn't part of the plan. What if Bran meets someone who saw me buying the ticket?

That's unlikely, I know, and this is Bran. Best friend, aspiring investigative reporter, CNN intern-in-the-making. I'd walk through fire for this boy; the least I can do is ask some questions for him so he can possibly get the internship he wants.

"Okay," I say, forcing a smile onto my face. "See you in an hour."

He heads into the crowd, and I turn away, walking toward the "Two Witches and a Kettle" popcorn tent.

"Hi there," I say, stepping into the tent. Two middle-aged Black women stand behind a table at the back of the tent. Although they wear matching flannels and jeans, one is tall, slim, and has shoulder-length red curls; the other is short and plump with frizzy gray hair. I'm not sure what I was expecting, but "witches" had me picturing more pointy hats and less soccer moms.

"Can I get a small caramel corn?" I ask. I'm the only customer in the tent, and my mouth waters as the smell of warm sugar and butter washes over me.

"Sure, hon," says the red-haired woman. "You need anything else?"

"Nope, that'll be all." Then I look guiltily down at the list of questions in my hand. "Well, actually, I was hoping to ask you some questions about the lotto winner."

The woman's eyes narrow. "Why? Are you a reporter? Somebody said there'd be reporters buzzing around, trying to get the story. But I told my wife, Cheryl"—she points to the shorter woman filling my bag of caramel popcorn—"we should just leave that poor person alone. Surely they've got enough problems without everybody in town trying to find them."

Amen.

I want to throw my arms around the woman and tell her she's absolutely right, but then her wife, the gray-haired Cheryl, comes up with my kettle corn. I fish a crumpled dollar out of my pocket and hand it over.

"Stop being such a dragon, Bea," says Cheryl. She pushes a few wisps of gray hair behind her ear. "What is it you wanted to ask?"

"I'm not a reporter," I say, gesturing to the ludicrous fedora on my head. As if that signifies anything. "But my friend, Bran, wants to be one. He's hoping to find the lotto winner, and I'm helping him out."

"I saw him on the news," says Bea. "So you're from around here and helping your friend?"

It's like she's asking for my passport or something. Proof of being a local and therefore worthy enough to hear her story.

"Yes, ma'am," I said. "I've lived here for five years, but my grandparents have been here for decades, or at least they were before my grandpa died and my grandma moved to Madison last year. Anyway, would you mind if I ask you a few questions?"

"Not at all. Fire away," says Cheryl with a much friendlier tone. She pulls a bag of kettle corn mixed with candy corn from her pocket and starts munching on it.

I start with the last question because it seems like the best one to get Bea and Cheryl talking: "What would you do with the money, if you had won it?"

Cheryl takes a long sip from a mug on the table and shakes her head. "Well, let's start by saying that we didn't win it. Though Lord knows we tried. I buy ten tickets a week when the jackpots get big. Always from Wanda's, and I was even in there on the day the ticket was bought."

"Same," says Bea. "The cards were reading really well for luck on Wednesday, so I dropped a hundred dollars on tickets."

Eeesh. I only spent one dollar on my ticket and its randomly generated numbers. It truly was a gift from the universe, the gods of chance, and circumstance. I wonder how close in time my ticket buying was from Bea's and Cheryl's.

"So, I guess that covers most of my other questions," I say, glancing at the list. I circle back to my original question, which they'd still not really answered. "Are you comfortable saying what you'd do with the money?"

Cheryl shrugs. "Well, I don't rightly know what I'd do. I think I'd be overwhelmed at first."

"It's a lot of money," adds Bea. "Entirely life changing, and I'm not sure I'd be ready for that kind of change all at once."

I find myself nodding in agreement, and it's all I can do not to burst out with my secret. Gah. Maybe I should ask Cheryl and Bea to cash the ticket for me.

Ridiculous, of course. I don't even know them.

Bea continues, "But I think we'd find a way to make it work. We've always wanted to travel, and neither of us were able to have kids. We've talked about adopting, but it's expensive."

A sad look passes over her face, and Cheryl wraps an arm around her wife. Good grief, maybe I really should ask them to cash the ticket. How would they take it? Would they actually give me some of the money and keep my secret? Could I trust them? This could help them achieve their dreams. But if I go around granting the wishes of every stranger I meet, I'd be broke before the day was out.

At that moment, a loud crowd of kids and some frazzled-looking parents step into the tent, interrupting my thoughts and wrenching Bea's and Cheryl's attention away from me.

"I want rainbow flavor!" yells one kid, pushing past me to snatch a bag of kettle corn off the table in front of me.

"I'm sorry," says the child's mom, pulling the kid back. She sets the bag on the table.

With a smile at Bea and Cheryl, I step aside. "It's okay. I'm done. Thank you both for talking with me."

Cheryl waves at me as she starts handing out samples to the kids, and Bea shoots me a wink. "You keep looking. I'm sure that lotto winner is around here somewhere."

"I bet you're right," I say as I take one of their business cards and slip out of the tent.

AN HOUR LATER, I'VE EATEN THE ENTIRE BAG OF KETTLE CORN, A toffee apple, and three street tacos from a food truck. My stomach aches, and I'm slumped against an oak tree near the bandstand, scrolling through a list of quotes from unhappy lotto winners on my phone:

Billie (Bob) Harrell, Jr., who won $31 million and later shot himself in the head: "The lottery is the worst thing that ever happened to me."

Sandra Hayes, who split a pot of $224 million with her coworkers: "I had to endure the greed and the need that people have . . . That caused a lot of emotional pain. These are people who you've loved . . . and they're turning into vampires trying to suck the life out of me."

Or Donna Mikkin, who won $34.5 million: She called herself "a happy person" before she won, but later said, "My life was hijacked by the lottery."

None of these quotes are encouraging, and I close my eyes for a moment to shut out the voices of the lotto winners in my head. The band starts up, and the crowd by the bandstand cheers its approval. What would knowledge of my win do to the people I know? Would they be cool with it, or would it turn them into vampires and emotional remoras? How many of the people at this festival would attack me if they knew I had the ticket tucked away at home?

"You okay, Jane?" says a familiar voice. Bran. He's always walking up to me when I'm spaced out like a weirdo these days. Sigh. Gotta get my shit together.

I snap my eyes open and quickly dismiss the window I was reading on my phone. "I'm fine. My stomach hurts a bit. What did you find out?"

Bran lets out a long breath and sits down beside me. "Well, everybody has lots of ideas about what they'd do with the money. But nobody seems to have any clue who actually won."

"That's pretty much what I found out too," I say, not adding that I didn't interview anyone besides Bea and Cheryl. "Most people were distracted by the festival, though I think a lot did buy tickets from Wanda's that day."

Bran picks at his fingernails, which he always does when he's thinking.

"So, what's the plan?" I ask. "Want to keep interviewing people?"

Bran doesn't get a chance to reply, because a loud scream cuts through the music. We jump to our feet and spin around.

At a craft booth a few feet away from us, two white women, one in a pink camouflage jacket and the other in orange leggings and a pumpkin sweatshirt, pull fiercely at a wreath. The wreath is actually a toilet seat that's covered in doll's heads, and it has to the be worst small-town craft I've ever seen. But that's not stopping these women.

"I saw it first!" yells Pink Camo. She jerks the toilet seat toward her body.

"It's mine," Orange Pumpkin shouts. "It's just like you to make a fuss about this. You KNOW I saw it first."

Bran meets my eye, and I nod. We are definitely getting closer to this action. We hurry toward the women, who seem oblivious to the crowd growing around the vendor's tent.

The seller, a young blond woman in a blue apron, tries to separate the other women, but they keep fighting over the toilet-seat wreath. I'm not even kidding. These women really want this monstrosity.

"You can't have it!" shouts Pink Camo. "This is just like that lotto-ticket winner. You're being selfish and keeping it to yourself."

"If I had the lotto ticket, I would keep it to myself!" Orange Pumpkin gives a mighty tug.

What happens next is the stuff of comedy routines and movie hijinks.

Orange Pumpkin lady pulls so hard on the toilet-seat wreath that Pink Camo loses her grip. But Orange Pumpkin has momentum, and she flies backward with a loud screech. The band stops playing and everyone turns as she smashes into a table covered in more wreaths (made from all sorts of household junk) and other quirky crafts. Glass shatters, and the table collapses under her weight, and then she rolls into one of the canopy poles holding up the tent. Bran and I step back as a gust of wind sends the entire canopy flying. It slams into the stall next to it, making that one crumple and sending shoppers scrambling.

My hand covers my mouth to stop the laugh that threatens to burst out of me, and the crowd takes a step back as Pink Camo strides over to the other woman and snatches the wreath from her hands.

"Selfish jerk," she shouts. "You're not getting this, and I wouldn't give you the lotto money, either! Even if I had won it!"

Pink Camo throws a twenty-dollar bill (twenty bucks! For a toilet-seat wreath!) at the seller and then storms away, still muttering to herself.

"What exactly happened there?" Bran asks as we start to pick up spilled crafts.

"Put that down," the seller snaps. "I can't have you kids stealing something on top of all this.

"We weren't going to steal—" Bran starts to say.

"Forget it," I say. "This lotto ticket is making people lose their shit. Let's go."

Leaving the seller, who's now arguing with the lady in the pumpkin sweatshirt, we move toward where Bran's car is parked.

"You want to stick around?" I ask. The band is playing again, but everyone seems shaken. "Maybe people will actually come to blows over the lotto ticket yet. Could be exciting."

Bran shakes his head. "I'm going to head home. I'm Skyping with Sofie soon, and I need to rethink my investigation protocol."

"I'll keep my eyes open."

Bran side-eyes me. "Or you'll go to the lake with Holden."

"Or I can do that. Clearly I'm a masochist, because this is a bad idea, right?"

Bran adjusts his fedora. "It's a terrible idea. But it's your life and your heart. You don't need my permission to do with it what you will."

I know that, of course. But after all the time Bran spent helping me get over Holden, I feel like I owe him an explanation, at least. "He's being cool, Bran. Maybe he's changed and really wants to get back together?"

Bran shrugs. "Just be careful. It hasn't been very long since you broke up. Make sure this isn't a rebound or something."

Can you rebound with the person who broke up with you? Is that bouncing back or falling down?

I have no idea. Which seems to be my operative state these days. Fuck. I have to figure out some of the mess that is my life. And quickly.

Silence that's not actually silence, because it's filled with the cheers of the crowd as the first riffs of a Bruce Springsteen song rise from the bandstand stage, stretches between Bran and me.

"I'll call you later," I promise. "And here, take this. Please." I hand the pink-and-blue fedora back to him.

Bran gives me a hug that I want to lean into because it feels like the only safe space in this town full of people whom I know so well, but whom I suspect would tear me apart for my money if they knew about the unsigned ticket in my bedroom.

CHAPTER TWELVE

THE SUN IS SETTING BY THE TIME HOLDEN PULLS AN OLD silver-and-maroon pontoon boat up to the public dock. It took me half an hour to walk to this side of the lake from downtown and another fifteen minutes to summon the courage to text Holden. I've been sitting on the dock, letting my sneakers skim the water, as I wait for him. I'm both nervous and excited as the boat bumps up, and I jump to my feet.

"I didn't think you were going to come," Holden calls out.

He's wearing jeans and a zip-up sweatshirt. Behind him, the sunset reflects on the water, breaking apart in the waves from the boat. The storm clouds from earlier are thunderheads above us now, but it's still not raining.

"I almost didn't," I say, taking the hand he offers me as I step onto the boat.

It's a familiar space, since I spent a lot of the last two years here, reading, swimming, and making out with Holden, but I haven't been on the boat since before Holden went to camp last summer. It feels good to be back on the lake. Some people are only steady on land, but for me, I'm most myself when I'm on the water. It's like some core component of me slots into place with the waves.

"I'm so glad you did," says Holden. I almost believe he means it.

My hand lingers in his, and I take a step forward. Right at that moment, the boat bobs to the left, tilting my body into Holden's. His arm slides around my back to steady me.

"Hi," he says softly, as his arm tightens around the curve of my hip.

"Hi," I reply, my lips an inch from his.

"Have I told you yet how much I like your short hair?"

I inhale sharply as his head tilts down toward mine. I move the smallest bit closer, and then we're kissing, just like old times. Holden's lips are slightly chapped, and as mine press into his, a rush of heat fills me.

I wish I could say it's terrible. But it's really not. And I don't hate it. But still, I wrench myself away.

"Shit. Sorry." I take a step back. "I didn't mean for that to happen. I know we're over, really. I swear I do." My voice stumbles over the words, as if I'm admitting them reluctantly.

I force myself take a deep breath and let it out slowly. So I kissed my ex. No big deal. Won't happen again.

"Old habits," says Holden, looking embarrassed. "I'm sorry too. Not that I haven't been thinking about doing that for days . . . It's just not like that between us now. I know. I messed everything up . . ."

Another gust of cold wind whips across the lake, and I shiver in my thin jacket, T-shirt, and jeans.

"It's not a big deal." I sit down on one of the benches and cross my arms. "We won't do it again. Promise."

Holden shoots me a look. "Deal. Hey, I have something for you. From my trip to Hawaii."

I shake my head. "You already gave me a pin, remember? Plus, you don't have to buy your ex-girlfriend gifts while you're on vacation."

"I know we were broken up at the time, but I saw it, and it screamed 'Jane!' at me. Do you want it?" He pulls a blue sweatshirt out from a grocery bag that's sitting on one of the seats. It has a humpback on it and says *Whale Watcher.*

Maybe if I wasn't shivering, I could say no. Sending him a small, grateful smile, I slip it over my head. It fits perfectly and smells like Holden's laundry detergent.

"I love it," I say, warming up from more than the fleece inside. "Thank you."

Holden returns my smile. That reckless bit of attraction that drew us together in the first place is still between us, practically a living thing. Dammit.

I look away first, trying to keep some part of myself unentangled. The sun is nearly down, and strains of music from the Harvest Festival drift out over the lake.

"Want to join the party?" Holden asks quietly as he turns the boat around. He nods toward the group of boats clustered near the beach. It looks like half my high school is there, drinking and hanging out.

"Nope." I point toward the middle of the lake far from the beach. "Let's get away from the crowd."

"Excellent plan."

Holden steers us away from the dock, and I close my eyes as the wind races over my face. It takes with it any thought of how stupid it was to kiss Holden—that just kind of happened, as these things go—and how nice it would be to kiss him again. The pontoon is no speedboat, but it's fast enough to make me forget anything but wind and water.

Holden stops when we're on the far side of the lake, closer to the marsh. Luckily, the mosquitoes have given up the ghost for the season, but I still pull the sweatshirt hood over my ears. Holden sits next to me, scooting close enough on the small-boat bench seat so our thighs touch. The waves rock us, and it takes everything in me not to lean my head onto his shoulder. Above us, the sky darkens, and thunder rumbles.

"So, how are college applications going?" I ask, seizing on the first neutral topic of conversation that floats through my mind. "Are still you planning on going somewhere near Lakesboro?"

As far as I knew, Holden wanted to go to UW–Madison, just like his parents had done. He'd always been into math, and that's what helped him get into the FICA camp last summer.

Holden makes a dismissive noise. "Not if I can help it. I want to get to New York City and stay there until I'm living above Central Park."

"Are you going to major in finance?" That had been his plan since we were sophomores and he'd started investing all his saved birthday money in stocks.

"Absolutely," says Holden. He picks at a piece of vinyl that's cracking on the boat seat and throws it overboard. "I'm done with shitty little towns, shitty festivals, shitty boats. All of it."

"How perfectly *Wolf of Wall Street* of you," I say dryly.

Holden laughs. "Tell me you wouldn't want to hang out on a yacht over this crappy boat?"

Of course some part of me wants to hang out on a yacht someday, but the rest of me wants to lecture Holden on the environmental impact of luxury yachts.

"What really happened in New York?" I blurt out. It's the question I've been turning over for the last two months. "I mean, you went away, like, this nerdy math guy who was casually interested in investments, and you came back caring about things like the Hamptons and yacht prices. I mean, it's fine, you can tell me: Were you body-snatched by a super materialistic alien?"

Holden barks a laugh, but it's sharp. With edges that dig into my bones. "I promise you I'm not an alien." He stares out over the lake for a moment and then runs a hand through his hair. "And truthfully, New York was fucking terrible. I went in thinking I could learn about Wall Street and find a place for myself there, but from day one, the other kids hated me. It's like I couldn't get the stink of Lakesboro off me, and they made fun of me for everything from my haircut to my clothing. They called me 'Holden from the Holler,' and to them, I was just some country bumpkin who was visiting the big city. Most of them made it quite clear I would never be their equal."

"But you *are* their equal, and that's just classist," I say, making a face. "Like, yes, there are terrible rich people who shit in gold toilets, but that doesn't mean you have to let them get under your skin."

Holden snorts. "I met someone with a golden toilet."

"You didn't."

"Swear to God." Holden pulls up his phone and scrolls through the pictures on it until he comes to one of him standing by the Wall Street bull and bear statues with a preppy-looking white guy in a blue blazer. "This is my roommate, Finn. Eventually, he was one of the only ones who stopped making fun of me."

"Was it his private jet you went on?" I ask, thinking back to what Holden told Bran, Sofie, and me a few days ago.

"Yep." Holden scrolls through more pictures and stops on one of an actual golden toilet. "This is the golden toilet in Finn's Upper East Side apartment."

"Unbelievable. Did you use it?"

"Yes."

I snort. "Was it a revelation?"

"No. It was mostly just uncomfortable."

"And wildly unethical to have such a thing, given the fact that millions of people are starving all over the world."

Holden shrugs. "That too, I guess. But money can do good as well. Especially if you have a lot of it. I mean, look at the Bill and Melinda Gates Foundation."

It occurs to me that if I do somehow cash this lotto ticket, I could, indeed, spend millions on a toilet. Or do lots of good in the world.

"So, tell me more about Finn," I say. Later, I'll think about what I could do with this money. Right now, I just want to keep Holden talking. "Are you still friends?"

Holden shrugs. "Sort of. He's nice enough, once you get to know him. His mom runs one of the biggest hedge funds on Wall Street and his dad is a CEO of another investment firm. His parents own a whole floor of a building."

"A whole floor? What does that even mean?"

Holden swipes to another picture on his phone. This one is of a gorgeous dark-paneled library with a view of Central Park. "Exactly what it sounds like. Their apartment takes up the entire floor, and it's outrageous. Italian marble everywhere, a staff of people to clean things up, and their own pool on the roof. They also have houses all over the world."

"And that's the life you want?"

"It is."

Holden's family isn't rich, but they're solidly middle class. His mom is a nurse and his dad runs the local hardware store, which has been in the family for three generations. Sure, Holden has been working at the store since he was fourteen, but he's never wanted for anything, and he's got a room full of electronics.

I turn so I'm facing Holden. "But, I mean, you do know Finn's life is a fantasy, right? It's not all good, and that much money can bring so many problems."

Holden puts his phone into his sweatshirt pocket. "Yeah, but at least with that much money I can pay someone to fix my problems."

"Sure, okay. Rich assholes get away with all sorts of things every day. Don't be like them."

Holden turns so he's facing me too. Our knees touch, and he runs one finger along the top of my leg. "I'm not going to be *that* kind of rich guy, I promise. I was just thinking more along the lines of never having to worry about money again. Or if someone I love gets sick, I'll have enough money to help them. Or I'll be able to pay for Harper's college and my parents' retirement."

His touch sends shivers through me, but I try to focus on what we're talking about. "While also possibly having a golden toilet of your very own."

Holden laughs. "I'm *not* going to get a golden toilet. But I will live well, see the world, and help people too."

These aren't the worst reasons for wanting to be rich. What would happen if I gave Holden the lotto ticket? Would he blow it all on a yacht? Could he actually bring himself to give me the money? Or even if we split the money, would it be so bad to help make some of his dreams come true?

Silence stretches between us for a long moment.

"I still can't believe you broke up with me because some kids you'll probably never see again were mean to you," I say, breaking the silence. As soon as the words are out, I want to push them back in.

Holden winces, as if my words actually slapped him. "I'm sorry about that, Jane. I really am. I came back super confused and feeling like I wanted more than what I had."

"But we were good, weren't we?"

"We were." He slips his hand into mine.

As I snake my fingers through his, I have to wonder: Can I trust him to not break my heart again?

I don't know, but I suspect Holden is the type of person for whom having some small part of happiness is never enough. I think he'll always want more stuff, more friends, more excitement, more lovers, and more money. But can having more stuff or more people or more experiences truly make a person happy? Or will they always be moving on to the next new thing?

I don't know the answer to any of those questions. But they're certainly ones that have been keeping me up at night, as I've considered whether cashing the lottery ticket will bring me happiness or misery.

"So, not to change subjects too much," Holden says softly, his body leaning into mine as the boat sways. "But it's wild about that lottery ticket, isn't it?"

I jolt away, pulling my hand out of his. It's too much like he's reading my mind. "Yeah, it's unbelievable."

"Is Bran still investigating?"

I try to steady my breathing, willing myself not to give anything away. "He is, and I'm helping a bit. I was asking around at the festival tonight."

"Find anything yet?" Holden's voice is eager, laced with curiosity or something else.

I don't know what to tell him. There's really nothing to tell at this point, other than my own secret. And I'm not ready to spill that yet. Before I can get my thoughts together, a crack of lightning splits the night.

"Oh shit," Holden exclaims. "That was really close. We should—"

The boom of thunder that follows drowns out his voice.

And then the sky opens up like someone overturned a huge bucket of water. Holden and I both jump to our feet.

"We've got to get off the lake!" I yell. Rain lashes at me.

Holden is at the steering wheel, firing the boat back up. Rain beats against the pontoon boat, making a metallic staccato that sounds like gunfire. I grip one of the side poles as Holden spins the boat around.

"Please don't let us die on the lake," I mutter to myself as another fork of lightning illuminates the sky. From downtown, the tornado sirens roar to life, screeching above our heads. My phone beeps in my pocket with an emergency warning. I read the alert quickly, swiping rain out of my eyes.

"Severe storms and flash floods!" I shout to Holden over the noise of the sirens and rain. He nods grimly, steering us toward the dark shoreline. The clump of boats where our classmates were hanging out has broken up, and other crafts zip across the lake, making the conditions like trying to cross a freeway during rush hour.

Somehow, we make it back to the dock. I jump out of the boat as soon as it pulls up, grabbing the rope on the bow. Holden is a step behind me, turning off the engine, and then he leaps onto the dock as well. Rain pounds into us, and the thunder crashes above.

"My car's over there!" shouts Holden above the noise of the storm.

We get the boat tied up and run for the car. The rain still pours from the sky, unrelenting. The water is already accumulating in the parking lot, but Holden unlocks his car, and we clamber in.

A great well of laughter rises up in me as another crack of thunder rips through the night.

"That was terrifying!" I say, catching my breath. I turn toward

Holden, adrenaline pulsing through me.

He's looking at me, his blue eyes lit up by another crack of lightning. My hands cup his face, reaching out for skin/human/something/anything to remind me that I'm not dead on the water.

I pull him toward me as he leans over to kiss me.

"Jane," he whispers against my mouth as our kiss deepens.

It's so familiar. So sweet. So much heat and intensity.

Holden's hands slip under my sweatshirt, finding my skin, and I start to pull off my shirt, but then the glare of red-and-blue lights fills the car.

"Shit," I mutter as a cop runs up to the window. He knocks twice, and Holden and I jerk away from each other.

Holden rolls the window down an inch or so, and rain blows into the car.

"What are you two doing?" the cop shouts. "Get home now! It's a flash-flood warning."

And then he runs back to his car.

Holden turns to look at me, and I shrug, not sure what to say, but giddy from the rain, our kiss, and the fact that the cop didn't arrest us for making out in public.

"I think I need a ride home," I say, gesturing toward the road. "I probably can't walk there in this weather."

Holden laughs and starts the car, and slowly we drive through the rain-sliced world, past the wreckage of the Harvest Festival, and toward my house.

CHAPTER THIRTEEN

WHEN I FINALLY MAKE IT HOME, I CHECK THE TOWN'S FACEBOOK group. No one has posted about the lotto winner, though there is a long thread about the Harvest Festival (the town is rightfully shocked that a toilet-seat wreath caused so much trouble).

A door opens somewhere in my house, and Mom moves around. She doesn't knock on my door, which is a relief. My head is full of Holden's lips on mine, our conversation, the terror of racing across the lake in a storm, and a general unease about the lotto ticket.

I let out a long, slow breath and twist the strings of my sweatshirt around my fingers. The cold dampness of the shirt—I'm still wearing the one Holden gave me—hits me. I really shouldn't be sitting around in this. Stripping off my wet clothes, I slip into dry pajamas and wrap myself in the comforter from my bed.

Then I do what I always do when I'm feeling too much: go to Facebook and find my dad's profile.

Yes, he's been dead for five years, but before that, he used social media like the rest of us. Mom never deleted his page—I don't even know if she knows the password—so it's out there for anyone to see. He's there, in a ghostly digital sense, whenever I need him. I wonder if in a hundred years no one will use Facebook or Instagram, but all our accounts will still be there, long after we're dead, like a great digital ship, full of our ghosts.

With a shivering breath, I click onto my dad's profile—Daniel Belleweather—and suddenly there he is: glasses, curly dark hair, lopsided smile like mine. His cover photo is of him, Mom, and me at Disney World, shortly before he died. Behind us, the Epcot ball rises like an enormous full moon. In this picture, I'm twelve, wearing glittery gold Minnie ears and grinning. Mom's got a hand on Dad's shoulder, and her hair is in a neat bob. There's nothing of the scattered, desperate, lonely collector of other people's memories in her face. There's nothing that hints at the fact that Dad would be dead a month after this picture was taken.

That Disney trip is one of my happiest memories with my parents, but these pictures are always hard. I scroll through my dad's Facebook feed, where all the posts are a few years old. There are a bunch of grief posts from people we used to know in Nashville. Neighbors, his college buddies, fellow firefighters. But I skip those and go back to the last post he made. August 10, 2016: He put up a picture of me and him on the Pirates of the Caribbean ride. I'm grinning, and he's giving me bunny ears. Mom took the picture from the seat in front of us. His caption: *YO-HO-HO, sailing the seven seas with my favorite ladies!*

I can still feel that small boat underneath us, bobbing along the ride, floating past towns that were fake burning and animatronic pirates guzzling booze, shooting at one another, and chasing people. It wasn't my first time on a boat, but I think that ride was the first time I knew I wanted to adventure on the sea. Not as a pirate (duh), but as a researcher. I think my dad would've liked that.

"Hi, Dad," I say, running a finger over his face on the screen. Tears fill my eyes, and I have to change the picture to the next one.

It's a selfie of us eating gelato at Italy in Epcot. Mom has her arm around me and we're smiling broadly. Dad's holding the camera, so his head looks huge, and his cherry gelato melts down his hand. The picture after that is of us in front of Space Mountain, where Dad puked his guts out and Mom and I rode three times in a row. The last picture, the one I always stop on, is of him and me by ourselves, standing on the edge of the Epcot lagoon at night. Mom took it from behind, so it's just our silhouettes, illuminated by the fireworks. My head leans on Dad's shoulder, and his arm is around me.

Even after all this time, I can't believe he's never coming home. That he'll never see me off to prom or walk me down the aisle at my wedding or ever tell me another bad dad joke. It's unthinkable that there's not enough money in the world to bring him back. That nothing will ever go back to the way it used to be.

I hate that so much.

Swiping at the tears in my eye, I click open the Facebook Messenger window that holds the conversation I've been having with my dead Dad for the last few years. I already know what my last post from back in August says, but I can't help but read it again.

August 19

Hi, Dad. It's now been five years and two days since you died. I miss you for so many reasons, and it's too bad you're not here. My boyfriend, Holden, just broke up with me a few days ago, and I really could use a shoulder to cry on. Or someone to punch him in his stupid face. Though I suppose I could do that, but then I'd have to see him again. We dated for two years. But then he got bored or something. I guess I wasn't enough. Sure, his excuse was that he "just needed some space," but I think that means he wanted to see other people. I don't know, and maybe

I don't care. But it hurts. So fucking badly. I feel like there's an eel eating my insides.

Remember when you told me, "Never let one person be the only person in your life"? I've tried to keep that in mind as I started dating, but it seems like most people in high-school relationships at least want you to be their one and only. Maybe I wanted that too. I think I just wanted to be special to someone. To be their everything. To know they weren't going anywhere. But clearly I wasn't enough for Holden. Which I know is not the end of the world—I'm only seventeen, I'll meet other people, but. Gahhh.

Remember when you told me, "The world is huge; go see it"? I think of that all the time, too. But I'm so afraid to leave this town. Even though I have things I want to do in the world. It's stupid to be ruled by fear. I know. But I still wish you were here. Mom's not doing well . . .

I stop reading. I haven't written anything since then, but tonight I need to talk to my dad. Typing to him is like screaming into the void, I know, but it still helps sometimes.

October 16

Hi, Dad. Guess what? Pretty soon, I'll officially be an adult. Remember how you told me that we'd go to Hawaii for my eighteenth birthday? I remember that. But that's not going to happen now, I know. Almost being an adult is weird. And it's only gotten stranger lately.

I pause over the keyboard, not sure how much I should say. But I need to tell someone. And it's not like Mom has read any of the other conversations in this message thread. None of the messages are marked as read, and surely if she had seen them somehow she would've asked me about some of the things in there—like me coming out as bi, or when I had sex for the first time, or when Holden broke up with me. Surely she would've given a shit about some of these things? Secrets are safe, it seems, as long as I tell them to the digital ghost of my dead dad.

I keep writing.

Want to know something unbelievable? I won the lottery. I really did. Right now, at this very moment, between the pages of my favorite book—*Sea Change*—is a lotto ticket worth $58 million. But the truth is, I don't know what to do with it. Oh, and also, since I bought it as a minor, I'm actually a criminal and can't cash it. So, I'm trying to figure that out right now. It's a mess. A hot mess of epic proportions.

What should I do, Dad? Everyone in town wants to know who won, and I just want to keep my secret until I find someone I trust to cash the ticket for me. But I don't know who that is. I know you'd say I can trust Mom, but she's so shaky right now. She's not been herself for a long time, and I'm not sure what she'd do with it.

I wish you were here.

I start to sign off, but then I remember one more thing I have to tell him that I can't tell anyone else.

Also, tonight I kissed Holden, a.k.a. that stupid boy who broke my heart two months ago. Actually, I kissed him twice. And it wasn't terrible. But what am I doing? Surely this is a sign that the lotto ticket is going to my head. But maybe I should give him another chance? What do you think?

I don't wait up for Dad's never-coming reply. I just crawl into bed with *Sea Change* clutched in my arms and pull the covers over my head.

CHAPTER FOURTEEN

M OM WAKES ME EARLY THE NEXT MORNING BY POUNDING ON MY
door. "Wake up, Fortuna Jane! We're going to Madison. Time
to go shopping!"

I make an incoherent noise and roll over. Mom keeps up the
pounding.

"Mom, it's Sunday. I'm sleeping. Go away!"

"Jane, I'm coming in there," she says, starting to push open the
door. I must have left it unlocked last night in my befuddled state.

I bolt up. "No! Mom, I'm up." I leap to my feet and slam the
door shut. I'm not sure why I do it. It's not like I have all sorts
of illegal stuff in here—no boys or girls I need to hide under my
bed (though, really, would Mom care?), no booze or drugs—I just
don't want Mom in here. Somehow if she comes in, it feels like the
sprawling mess of the rest of the house will follow her.

Mom lets out a long sigh on the other side of the door. It's a
sound that makes something in me crumple like a used tissue. This
distance between us is partially my fault, I know. I stand on my side
of the door, hand against it, heart racing from jumping out of bed.
Mom and I must look like bookends cradling a volume filled with
everything we can't say to each other.

"I'll be out in eight minutes," I call.

There's a moment of silence so long I wonder if Mom still stands on the other side of the door. Then she says softly, "I'll be in the truck. Bring a jacket. It's even chillier today than yesterday."

I turn away, my heart full of too many things, and pull on some jeans, a thick sweater, and my sneakers. With a glance at the time—6:54 a.m., way too early to be up on a Sunday—I shove my phone into my pocket and head to my bathroom. Usually I'd take a long, hot shower, especially after getting caught in the rain last night, but this morning I splash some water on my face and brush my teeth super fast. Mom honks the horn. After putting *Sea Change* back on the shelf, I grab my purse, lock my door on the way out, and then weave through the crowded house to the front door. The wedding dress mom pulled out of the trash a few days ago now hangs in the doorway between the living room and the kitchen. It's a great blob of a shape, and seeing it sagging there, the discarded shell of someone else's dream, makes me ache.

What I wouldn't give for a cup of coffee or, better yet, to have Dad in the kitchen, cooking breakfast and listening to jazz. I close my eyes for a moment, seeing him in our old kitchen on the day before he was killed in that fire at the apartment building with the gas leak. He'd made omelets and waffles for all three of us. I brush at the tears that rise, unbidden, to my eyes.

Mom honks again.

Sighing, I flick off the lights in the living room.

A few minutes later, Mom is speeding along Highway 94, headed west toward Madison. It's a beautiful fall day, and there are no signs of the storms that tore through here last night other than some fields that now resemble shallow lakes. I slug syrupy French vanilla coffee that I got at the convenience store as Mom filled up with gas. (Not Wanda's, because that place is still dark, shuttered, and closed.) We don't talk for most of the ride. I switch the radio on, and the soothing tones of NPR fill the car, but Mom snaps it off at once. She used to love listening to the radio, but now she surrounds herself with silence like she surrounds herself with other people's memories. Maybe if she just let in some music or some of her own memories, she wouldn't need all these others. I really should look up how to help her, but that seems beyond my scope so early in the morning.

"Where are we headed?" I ask as Madison comes into view. The dome of the capitol sits on an isthmus between two lakes. We're coming in from the east side of town, and the morning light paints Lake Monona with gold and pink brushstrokes. Today's a farmers' market day, so the Capitol Square will be crowded with people buying pumpkins, jars of jam, and all sorts of other local, seasonal goodies.

"St. Vinny's," she says at once, her eyes never leaving the road. "On Willy Street. Then we're meeting your grandmother at the farmers' market for lunch."

Seeing Grandma is a treat, but of course we're going to St. Vinny's first. It's the largest thrift store in town and one of Mom's favorites. Around this time of year, they have their Halloween costumes out, and it's always full of bizarre treasures. Mom is going to buy so much.

I Google St. Vinny's. "They don't open until nine, so we've got almost an hour. Want to get some breakfast?"

Mom doesn't look away from the street, where she's like an arrow pointed in the direction of the thrift store. "Sure, but we'll get it to go. I want to be the first ones through those doors when they open."

Of course she does. Fighting back a snarky comment, I direct Mom toward an artisanal bakery on Willy Street.

We eat our pastries on the steps of St. Vinny's. A gray-haired homeless man with a red, wind-burnished face shares the step with us, leaning against the corner of the building to sleep. He's wrapped in layers of coats, and I give him the extra ham-and-cheese croissant I'd bought for later. He smiles at me gratefully, and I wish I could do more. If I can find a way to cash this lotto ticket, then I could set up a shelter or a charity or do all sorts of good in the world, just like Holden and I talked about yesterday.

If, though.

If is the operative word here.

Because the only way I can do anything like that is IF I can find someone to say they bought the ticket and then give me the money.

I glance at Mom. She's peering in the thrift-store windows and checking her watch. She bounces on her toes impatiently as the minutes tick down to opening.

How could I even trust her with my secret? Much less all this money?

I just can't. There's no way.

Which leaves Grandma and Holden. I shove those thoughts away for now, as they're full of too many unknowns to contemplate this early in the morning.

Finally, at two minutes past nine, when Mom's ready to ram through the store door—sheets of glass and laws about property destruction be damned—a woman finally unlocks St. Vinny's.

Mom pushes past her, calling over her shoulder, "Hurry, Fortuna Jane! Grab a cart!"

I get to my feet slowly and follow Mom into the store.

Inside is a riot of secondhand clothes, Green Bay Packers

memorabilia, used books, old furniture, pots and pans, broken appliances, and all sorts of other junk. St. Vinny's takes up most of a city block, and it has lots of small rooms tucked into the space. Pulling a rickety silver cart from a tangle of baskets near the registers, I trail behind Mom as she navigates a corridor between shelves covered in ceramic figurines and coffee mugs.

She darts toward a coffee mug with a smiling toddler on it, as if she can't help herself, but then she whispers, loud enough that I can hear, "Focus, Joy Lynn. We're here for wedding dresses."

Oh my God.

We're here for wedding dresses.

Of course we are.

It takes everything in me not to abandon the cart right then and there.

Mom marches ahead, heading straight into the enormous Halloween section, which fills a room larger than my school cafeteria. A rainbow of prom dresses covers an entire rack, and I can't help but run my hands along the sequins and silky fabrics. Mom strides on, stopping only when she gets to the wedding dresses, which fill the end of an aisle like enormous exploded meringues on *The Great British Bake Off*.

I pull a turquoise silk dress with a halter neck and no back off the rack. It's solidly out of, like, 1997, and it falls to the ground in an ombré of blues that remind me of waves and the ocean. Or Holden's eyes. For a moment, I let myself imagine going to prom with him. Or us hanging out after prom and going to a party at the beach . . .

My phone chimes with a text.

BRAN: Where are you? Are you still alive after that storm last night?

JANE: I'm alive, though I got caught on the lake during the storm.

BRAN: With Holden?

JANE: Yes, but it was no big deal.

BRAN: I don't believe you. Where are you?

JANE: In Madison with Mom. She's having a Miss Havisham moment.

I drop the turquoise dress on the rack and snap a selfie with mom in the background, pawing through the wedding dresses, and send it to Bran.

BRAN: Wait. Is she buying wedding dresses? What are you not telling me? Is your mom getting married? Or did Holden propose? Because I'm a supportive BFF, but there's no way you're marrying that guy.

JANE: Snort. That's exactly it. How did you know?

BRAN: LOL. Told you I had investigative skills.

JANE: You do indeed. And before you ask, nothing is going on between Holden and me. We just hung out for a bit.

Which is not exactly the truth, but there's no reason to alarm Bran via text about my kissing habits.

BRAN: Uh-uh. I deduce you're lying about that, but I'm here when you're ready to talk.

JANE: Thank you. Hey, any new leads on the lotto winner?

I really, really hate myself for asking him about that. It's such a blatant move away from deep emotional waters, and how could he have any more leads? I'm still here, holding onto the unsigned ticket and lying to him.

I swear, when I find a way to cash this ticket, I'm going to do something incredible for Bran.

BRAN: Nothing yet. I'm keeping an eye on the Facebook

group, hoping someone says something. Also emailed Wanda, but I haven't heard back yet.

"Jane! Come help me!" Mom screeches from the end of the aisle. There's a great clattering as the rack she was riffling through collapses and a dozen wedding dresses fall on top of her.

JANE: Gotta go! Mom's just been buried by a wedding-dress avalanche.

I snap another quick picture of the mountain of tulle and lace, with Mom's hand thrust out of it, and send it to Bran.

BRAN: ☺ Let me know if you need me to come pick you up.

JANE: If we're here for more than three hours, I'll call you for a rescue. xoxo.

MOM WANTS TO BUY ALL THE DRESSES.

When I finally pull her out of the pile (she emerges a bit breathless and with a flourish, kind of like a stripper jumping out of a cake), she stacks them all into our cart.

"We can't get every dress, Mom," I say. I tug a fluffy dress that looks like something from the '80s out of the pile and flip over the tag. "This one is twenty dollars and"—I flip over another price tag—"this one is twenty-five. For all fifteen dresses, you're looking at, like, three hundred dollars." Carefully, I pull another dress out of the cart and hang it on the closest unbroken clothes rack.

Mom lets out a frustrated breath. "I know that, Fortuna Jane. But we *need* these."

A high-pitched laugh escapes me. "We don't. In fact, we absolutely do not need any of these dresses at all."

"We do! These are someone's memories, about to be snatched away by an uncaring public!"

"How much money do you have on you?"

Mom crosses her arms. "None of your business."

"It is my business. I only have thirty dollars on me. You?"

"Fifty," Mom says. Her voice now has a frantic edge, like she is doing some terrible mental contortions to make the small sum stretch to cover all the dresses. And pretty much everything else in the store.

"And we need to get gas and lunch."

"Nonsense. Your grandmother will pay for lunch."

"Mom. You know we can't afford all these dresses."

An agonized look crosses Mom's face. "But, Jane. We *need* them."

Before I can reply, a white twentysomething woman in a ratty sweatshirt and torn jeans taps me on shoulder. "Excuse me," she says. "Are you buying all those wedding dresses?"

"Yes," Mom says, pulling the cart toward herself.

"No," I say. "Take your pick." I pull the rest of the dresses out of the cart and put them back on the rack.

"Thank you," the woman says gratefully. "I'm getting married soon, and I'm going to take one of these and modify it." A smile curves the edges of her mouth as she goes through the dresses.

"See," I whisper to mom. "Other people will make memories with those dresses. That's why you can't take them all."

Mom snatches one dress off the rack. "I'm getting this one," she mutters to herself as I steer her away from the wedding dresses, leading her to the other side of the store.

I take the dress from her gently, turning it over. It has long lace sleeves and a high collar.

"I married your father in a dress like this," she says, her voice so soft I almost can't hear it.

I know this is true because a wedding photo of them used to hang in the living room. Maybe it's still there, buried underneath all the photos of other people.

Tears rise in my eyes. I can let her have this, at least. "It's lovely. Let's get it."

Mom shoots me a grateful look and then makes an excited noise. Her fingers grip my arm. "Janey, look at that! Who in the world would donate such a thing?"

She points toward the back of the store, where an oil painting of two kids hangs. The girl wears a blue dress, and the boy has on a suit. It's clearly the kind of thing a doting parent had commissioned, but how did it end up here?

The tender moment where we actually talk about our feelings disappears as Mom throws the old wedding dress in the cart and hurries toward the portrait. She's back in her element, diving right into filling the holes in herself with other people's cherished things.

We get the painting, the dress, a freezer-size Ziploc bag of old photos, and a cross-stitched monstrosity that is all about being a mother-in-law (that someone's mother-in-law clearly hated enough to donate).

Somehow Mom talks the clerk into discounts on it all, and she still has money left.

"I'm going to check out that estate sale a few blocks over," she says cheerfully as we pile everything into the truck. "Want to come?"

I absolutely do not. Thrift stores and pulling things out of the trash are one thing, but walking through someone's home after they've died in order to scoop up the remains of their material possessions is high on the list of most depressing things I can think of. I get that it's a great way to find cool things or upcycle, but the sight of a crushed-velvet armchair that still has an imprint from its previous owner's butt, and the sense that the owner recently vacated the chair, the house, and the world, is just too much for me.

"Pass," I say. "I'm going to go find Grandma at the farmers' market. Text me when you're on your way, and we'll meet you back at her condo."

"It's a long walk to the capitol," says Mom from the front seat of the truck. "Want a ride?"

"Mom. It's, like, a mile. I'm fine."

She nods, her rare burst of maternal concern over. "Okay, see you in a while!" And then she guns down the street, pointed in the direction of the paper signs that scream *ESTATE SALE!*

Pulling out my phone, I text Grandma to tell her I'm on my way, put on my headphones, and crank up some music as I head south down Willy Street.

CHAPTER FIFTEEN

GRANDMA WAITS FOR ME OUTSIDE A COFFEE SHOP ON CAPITOL Square. Beyond her, the view of Lake Monona stretches, blue and glittering in the October light. In front of us, the Dane County Farmers' Market circles the capitol building like a living wreath made up of booths and moving visitors. Usually it happens only on Saturday mornings, but happily, it's running an extra day this weekend. Some of the shoppers carry huge bouquets of late-season flowers, others pull wagons full of kids and pumpkins, some have baskets piled high with produce, and lots of couples stroll hand in hand, eating pastries and drinking coffee. There's a bubbling energy and sense of contentment that thrills me. It's like a grown-up version of Lakesboro's Harvest Festival, and it feels more real and exciting somehow than anything my tiny town could pull off.

"Hi, Jane!" calls Grandma, waving me over to her table. Today she wears a colorful long-sleeve caftan, yellow clogs, and her short gray hair is spiky. She looks exactly like the liberal, tree-hugging, art-museum docent of an old lady she is.

She stands up to hug me as I approach, and I sink into the hug. "Hi, Grandma," I say, trying to keep my voice neutral so I don't cry in front of her. Sometimes a huge sense of loss sneaks up on me, reminding me exactly how much I miss having Grandma living with us.

"Sit down, eat something," she says, letting go of me to gesture at the two cups of coffee on the table. "I ordered you a club sandwich on multigrain. That's still your favorite?"

"It is, thank you. But aren't we having lunch at your house? Mom's headed that way after she hits a few estate sales."

Grandma rolls her eyes. "It's a beautiful day, and the last thing I want is to sit inside while your mother—who's my daughter and whom I love very much—tells me how my place is too bare. She gets positively twitchy inside. I'll text her and tell her to come here."

I take a long sip of the coffee. "You noticed that too?"

"Yes," Grandma says. "Have you ever—"

A café employee comes up, carrying two baskets of food. He plops them on the table, smiles at me, and walks away.

Grandma doesn't finish her thought, and I don't ask her about it. We both know what she was going to say because we've discussed it all before: Have I ever thought about getting Mom some help? Is there anything Grandma can do? Can we really not just clear everything out of the house while she's at work?

My answers are always: Thanks for thinking of us; there's nothing you can do; and if we moved everything out all at once, it'd probably kill Mom, and then I'd be an orphan.

I take a huge bite of my sandwich while Grandma texts Mom and I people-watch for a few minutes.

"So, how's condo-commune life?" I ask once half my sandwich is gone.

Grandma grins. "Wonderful."

She points to the building where she lives. It rises fifteen stories, and her unit overlooks Lake Monona. It's not exactly the hippie commune she wanted, but she's working hard to make it that in her own way.

"The sunrises are beautiful, and I've made friends with several of the single gentlemen down the hall from me."

I roll my eyes. "What ever happened to 'don't shit where you eat'?"

"Language, Fortuna Jane," Grandma admonishes with a laugh. "And say what you will, but it keeps me young."

"No judgment here," I say. "I'm glad to have a grandma who's with the times."

"Amen," says Grandma. "Aging is hard enough without being forced to stay in your house, knitting and supposedly never thinking about sex again. Speaking of all that, how's your sex life?"

"Still none of your business, but also still nothing new to report."

There's no way she gets to hear about Holden now. I told her far too much when we were dating, including the fact that we were having sex, and I also called her crying the night Holden broke up with me. I can only imagine what she'd say if I told her I was hanging out with him again.

Grandma pats my hand. "You know I'm here to talk whenever you need me. The repressive taboo surrounding teenage sex is so harmful."

"I agree. But let's talk about something—anything—else. Please. What's going on in the world?"

I point to her newspaper. There's a picture of a girl in a knight's costume on the front page, along with an article about how she helped change gender restrictions at the medieval-themed restaurant where she worked and how she's now jousting at a Renaissance fair. I reach for the paper so I can read the piece, but Grandma gets to it first.

"Oh, yes!" she says, flipping through the pages. "I wanted to show you this. There's something in here about Lakesboro. And I think they quoted your friend."

She turns over the page, landing on an article that makes me choke on a bite of club sandwich. I take the newspaper from her and read:

LITTLE TOWN, BIG LOTTO WINNER

The small, rural community of Lakesboro was in for quite a surprise earlier this week when someone bought the winning Mega-Wins ticket from a local gas station. Worth over $58 million, the ticket was purchased from Wanda's Quick-Go Shop on Wednesday night. So far no winner has come forward, but the town is eagerly waiting to hear if they have a multimillionaire in their midst.

"My best friend and I have been asking around, but so far we have no leads," said Brandon Kim, a local teen who is working to find the lotto winner.

Others in the town have stronger opinions on whom it could be, and one local, who wished to remain anonymous, said recently, "It's a shame someone hasn't come forward. I think the police should get involved. Just so we can all stop worrying. Seems mighty selfish for the winner to keep all that money hidden . . ."

I stop reading the article, not wanting to hear what else people in my town think.

I look over at Grandma. "Yep, that's my friend Bran. He's trying to figure out who won so he can break the story."

"Any luck so far? I can imagine that much money might rip a town apart." Grandma takes a sip of her tea.

I shake my head. If ever there were a time to tell Grandma about the ticket, it's now. She could cash it, give me the money or split the winnings with me, and we'd be fine. Problem solved.

Taking a deep breath, I look at Grandma. "So, what would you do if you had that lotto ticket?"

Grandma makes a disgusted noise. "I'd never have the lotto ticket because you know I don't play the lotto! It's a fool's tax. I've told your mother that a thousand times, but she still keeps buying tickets."

"But let's just say you did have it somehow, what would you do?"

"Throw it away immediately! There's no part of me that wants that sort of drama and trouble."

"Grandma, you couldn't throw away $58 million."

She scoffs. "I most certainly could. Though you're right, I wouldn't throw it away. I'd cash it and then promptly give all the money to charity."

I goggle at her for a moment. "You wouldn't keep any of it?"

"Not a cent."

"That's outrageous."

Grandma shrugs. "That's what it is. I don't think money is the most important thing in life, and if someone handed me that much, I'd say thank you but no thank you."

Welp.

That answers one of my questions. I definitely cannot ask Grandma to cash the ticket. I mentally cross her off my list.

That just leaves Holden.

Nope, nope, nope, nope.

Bad choices all around.

I finish my sandwich, and then before we can talk about anything else, Mom walks up the street, carrying a severed head.

Okay. So it's not a real head.

It's the kind of bald mannequin head women put wigs on. But it's creepy AF, with its peeling-paint eyes and arched eyebrows. Mom plops it onto the table, like it's a fourth member of our party. Grandma and I share a look.

"Can you believe this was just being thrown away?" Mom exclaims as she sits down. "They gave it to me at the estate sale. Said the owner had it for sixty years and her mother gave it to her. Imagine the stories! This is where women kept the hair they wore on first dates, to weddings, to parties . . ." She trails off with a dreamy expression on her face.

"It's a disturbing plastic head, Mom," I say, wishing I could shove it under the table. Or better yet, into the trash. I scoot my sandwich far away from it.

"It's history, Fortuna Jane," says Grandma with a quick wink at me. Her voice is gentle, and I know she's trying to be kind to Mom, but it isn't really helping. "I'm glad you found it, sweetie. Can I get you some lunch?"

Mom pulls a pile of costume jewelry out of her bag and arranges it on the table. Pink, blue, yellow, and green paste gems sparkle in the sunlight from giant gaudy necklaces and earrings. "No need; I'm not hungry. But let me show you what else I managed to save."

Grandma and I share another look, and then we let Mom tell us about each brooch, pin, and photo she "rescued" from the estate sale.

As she talks, I watch kite surfers skim over the surface of Lake Monona, carried on the wind like leaves. From here, they look free and fearless, moving across the water with nothing holding them back. I yearn to trade places with them.

NEW POST BY AMY PEMBERLY: Well, folks, it looks like no one is coming forward as the winner of this ticket. Maybe they are out of state? Or maybe somebody is afraid? Just thought I'd start this thread as a place for us to talk about what we'd do if we had won. So, tell us: What would you do with the money?

MEGAN WILLIAMS: I'll go first. If I'd won the $58 million, I'd build a rec center in town for kids. It'd have gymnastics, a place for parents to hang out, and lots of fun activities.

AMY PEMBERLY: This is a great idea! Definitely would take my kids there!

LISA HAWKINS: ESPECIALLY IN THE WINTER!

[20 more comments]

KANDI TAYLOR: I love that idea of building something for the community, but I have to say I'd use the money to pay off all my school-loan debt and my mom's medical bills. Then, byyyee! I'd move to the tropics.

AMY PEMBERLY: Absolutely. Wouldn't it be amazing if the lotto winner did something like pay off all our medical bills?

J. WILKINS: Keep dreaming. That person doesn't even

have the courage to come forward. Why should they do something good for the community when they're now RICH? [78 more comments]

JOHN SANDERS: I'd use the money to create some sort of barrier that kept the smell from the chicken farms out of town. Good grief, it's bad tonight.

J. WILKINS: That's the smell of country life. Love it or leave.

MARGO LEWIS: Back to what we'd do with the money: If any of you are feeling generous, my four-year-old just got back from his first cancer treatment, and we don't have insurance. We have a GoFundMe. Or you could just send him a message here. I'll read them to him. Thanks!

TOM HOFFMAN: Speaking of GoFundMe pages, my best friend is a single mom and about to lose her house. She could really use some help. Here's the link.

AMY PEMBERLY: Hope the lotto winner sees this so they can help.

J. WILKINS: Fat chance. I tell you, that person is sitting on the money like Scrooge McDuck so they can keep it for themselves.

MARY FULTON: Sadly, I bet you're right. [58 more comments]

CHAPTER SIXTEEN

Wʜᴇɴ I ᴘᴜʟʟ ᴍʏ ʙɪᴋᴇ ɪɴᴛᴏ sᴄʜᴏᴏʟ ᴏɴ Mᴏɴᴅᴀʏ ᴍᴏʀɴɪɴɢ, ᴀ ʙᴜɴᴄʜ of kids from my senior class are already loaded into a school bus. We're going to the House on the Rock, and I'm later than usual because I overslept.

"Jane!" Holden shouts, leaning out the window. "C'mon. I saved you a seat."

I take off my headphones and wave to him. We haven't talked since Saturday night, a.k.a. that night we kissed on the lake and then again in the parking lot. Although I've been tempted to text him about fifty-eight million times.

Bran is already on the bus, but the seat next to him is taken. "I'm sorry," he says as I pass. "I tried to save you a seat."

"No worries," I say, squeezing his shoulder as I pass. "I'll survive."

The rest of the bus is full, so I slide into the seat next to Holden. It's only when I do that I realize I'm wearing the sweatshirt he gave me. Like a total creep. But, in my defense, it was on the floor near my bed, and it's Monday.

Sigh.

"Hi," he says, in a low voice that tugs at something deep in my belly. "I had fun on Saturday." His hand snakes around my waist, pulling me closer to him.

I shrug out of the embrace because we can't do that in public yet, can we? We're not dating. We're barely even hanging out. What does any of this with him even mean?

"I had fun too," I whisper. "Minus the getting caught in a flash-flood part."

Holden laughs and takes two granola bars out of his bag. "Breakfast?"

"That's surprisingly thoughtful of you," I say, taking one.

Bran looks back at me from a few seats up, glaring at Holden. I shrug and open the granola bar.

Our history teacher gets on the bus, calling for silence as she takes roll, and then the bus rumbles to life.

I offer Holden an earbud and put some music on my phone. While we drive the hour and a half to Spring Green, Holden shows me all the photos from his trip to Hawaii. I try not to be jealous, but it's impossible. There he is, smiling and nonchalant on the whale-watching tour his family took. Someday. I'll get there someday.

"Want to trade seats, Holden?" says Bran, walking back toward us after we've been chatting for a while.

"Mr. Kim! Take your seat!" our teacher screeches from the front of the bus. Bran rolls his eyes.

"We're pretty comfortable here," Holden says. "What do you think, Jane?"

I think I'm in way over my head with Holden, since I've been fighting the urge to kiss him for the last hour.

"Yes, trade seats," I say to Holden in a rush. "Bran and I have stuff to discuss."

"If that's what you want," Holden says with a crooked grin. He shrugs and steps past me. I slide into the seat he just left and press my cheek into the coolness of the window.

"What are you doing?" Bran demands as he sits down beside me.

I let out a tired, oh-so-exhausted breath. What *am* I doing? Almost missing field trips because I overslept? Flirting with Holden? Hiding the fact that I'm a multimillionaire from my best friend?

I just shake my head. "I don't know, but let's not talk about it right now."

It would be impossible to talk anyway, because Holden has traded seats again and now he sits behind us with a bunch of his cross-country buddies who are making loud, obnoxious jokes.

Bran raises one eyebrow. "Tell me there's nothing between you two."

"There's nothing between us. Just a lot of history. Now, will you please tell me the next steps in your investigation?"

That's all it takes to get Bran talking again. Soon, he's got a notebook out and is walking me through his carefully plotted, fifteen-step plan to find the lucky winner. I keep my cheek against the window, half listening, all the way to the House on the Rock.

THE HOUSE ON THE ROCK IS WEIRD. LIKE, TRULY, DEEPLY, MIND-bogglingly weird. Most of us in my class know it from the TV show (or the book, in my case) *American Gods*. But even that doesn't get at what it is to walk through hundreds of rooms full of tiny miniature circus figures, porcelain dolls, pneumatic machines, and everything in between. I've been once before, with Mom and Dad when I was very small. I remember thinking it was both magical and terrifying.

"The House on the Rock opened to the public in 1960," our teacher calls out as we stand in the hallway at the front of the house. "Alex Jordan's father purchased this land—some say in a bid to anger Frank Lloyd Wright, who lived ten miles away—and Alex devoted his life to making this house spectacular. Today I want you to wander through the house, and we will all meet for lunch in a few hours. Don't break anything, and please fill out your question sheets as we go. You will be getting a test grade for completing them."

She hands out long, stapled lists of questions. I glance at one: *Where did Alex Jordan live most of his life?*

"That one's easy," Bran whispers beside me. "I looked him up last night. He's from Madison and only spent four nights in this house."

"So strange," I reply. "Imagine having all this space and just filling it up. It's not a house; it's a museum."

Bran nods. "That's exactly what it is."

The parallel to my own home is not lost on me, but I don't say anything about it.

As our teacher drones on, giving us all instructions for staying safe and what to do if we get lost, I wonder: If I find a way to cash the lotto ticket, could I purchase something like the House on the Rock? Or create something like it myself? What will my legacy be after all these years?

"Was Alex Jordan rich?" I blurt out suddenly, louder than I mean to.

The class stops whispering, and my teacher stops talking.

Holden snorts. "Of course he was. Look at this place, Jane."

"I was just about to ask the same thing," Bran whispers. "It was a good question." He bumps his shoulder against mine. I want to hug him.

My teacher raises a hand to stop the laughs. "Actually, though this house is sprawling, it's hard to say whether Jordan was rich or not. He was notoriously reclusive, and he financed much of this place through giving tours of it."

That makes everyone stop talking for a moment. Imagine how many tours you'd have to give to build a place like this.

"Okay, everyone," our teacher says. "If there are no more questions, go forth and enjoy." She waves her hands in a wide swath. I can almost hear her racing for the parking lot to sneak in a smoke before she meets us somewhere deep in the bowels of the house. "And don't break anything! I mean it!"

"We won't," Holden calls out. There's a low wave of laughter from everyone else, and Holden, his cross-country friends, and most of the rest of the class head toward the Infinity Room.

Technically, the Infinity Room is neither a room nor something that stretches to infinity. It's more like a long hallway with a carpeted floor that has three thousand small, wood-framed windows along its sides and a bunch of ceiling fans going at full speed. It narrows to a point and juts out into the sky—unsupported—like the prow of a ship. Total hell for a claustrophobic soul like myself.

Bran and I stand at the entrance to the Infinity Room as students from our class dare each other toward the end. Someone squeals as the room sways in the October winds.

"No way am I going in there," I tell Bran. "Let's get exploring."

"Agreed," he says. "Plus, I think Holden and company are going to do something stupid, so let's stay as far away from them as possible."

I glance toward the far end of the Infinity Room, where Holden and his friends are now stomping heavily, trying to bounce the entire thing like it's a tightrope strung between trees. A stern-looking HOTR employee strides toward them, and I don't want to see how this all ends up. I suppose if I were still Holden's girlfriend, I'd be down there too, laughing along with everyone else. Or would I? Would I have let Holden influence me to do something so clearly against what I wanted?

I'm betting I'd be out here with Bran, which would've probably just pissed Holden off.

Right. Okay. So, now that I think of it, maybe we weren't a perfect rom-com couple. I remember a thousand small fights with Holden about exactly this sort of thing.

With a glance back at the students in the Infinity Room, Bran and I walk away from the original house part of the House on the Rock. We wind our way past dozens of stained-glass lights, dusty velvet couches, walls of weapons, and much, much more. There's a deep sense of nostalgia throughout, especially in sections like the Music of Yesterday or the life-size reproduction model town from the 1800s. In that fake town, Bran pauses in front of a nineteenth-century "miracle cures" display in a faux pharmacy window.

"This is gross," he says, pointing to the hundred-year-old tapeworm in a bottle. "It was sold to help women lose weight. Good grief."

"That's nasty," I agree, ready to keep walking. "Let's keep going."

We move farther into the darkness of the house, and while Bran stops to read a label on a display about haberdashery—because hats! Fedoras! Oh my!—I try to quell the anxiety that I can feel snaking through my body. It's making my heart race, and I need a quiet moment away from all this stuff.

"I'm going to find a bathroom," I say to Bran. I peer at our map. "There's supposed to be one somewhere around here."

"Good luck, and if I don't see you in an hour, I'll send a search party," says Bran.

I laugh and head down a hallway to our right, thinking about all the reasons why the House on the Rock creeps me out:

1) Because I have no idea how deep in the earth we are (remember, claustrophobic);

2) Because of the smell of mildew and the cacophony of music from all the mechanical orchestras is overwhelming my senses;

3) And, most of all, because it feels like I'm walking through my mother's brain.

Seriously, if her mind could be made into an object, it would look something like the House on the Rock.

Which is terrifying.

As with our house, here too much stuff is shoved into what was once a home. What would Mom do in a place like this? Would it feel welcoming to her? Like she'd found a kindred spirit in this person who was determined to save all this junk from certain extinction? Or would she be as overwhelmed as I am?

"Hey, Earth to Jane," a voice comes up from behind me.

Holden. He rests a hand lightly on my lower back.

I look up from the display case full of false teeth that I've stopped in front of while my brain churns. Bran is nowhere in sight, and I have no idea how long I've been standing here.

"Hey," I say.

"Super into false teeth?" Holden quirks a half smile.

I laugh, trying to shove my dark thoughts away. "I didn't want to tell you this, but they're fascinating. I'm thinking of starting my own collection."

Holden gives me a look like he can't figure out if I'm joking or not. I roll my eyes at him. "I'm kidding."

"Okay, good," he says, relief in his voice.

I'd forgotten how Holden likes to make a joke but doesn't always get the joke unless it's explained to him. Silence stretches between us.

"How's your worksheet going?" he asks, holding up his questions sheet. It's partially filled out.

"I haven't touched mine," I admit. "Have you seen Bran?"

Holden shrugs and gestures toward the part of the house we were in earlier. "I passed him wandering around back there somewhere, looking at his checklist and trying to call you."

I pull my phone out, but it has no bars. Hopefully I'll meet up with Bran soon. Holden and I begin to amble toward the next section of the house.

"So, what happened to Banks and Hunter and all your other cross-country dude-bro buds? I can't believe they let you wander around on your own."

Holden bumps me back. "I love how much you love my friends. They're not that bad, you know."

"Really? Have you met them?"

Holden laughs at that. "They're back there, daring one another to try on some suits of armor. I was looking for you, though. How are you doing?" His hand brushes mine as we walk, and I have the most foolish of urges to turn my body toward his and kiss him right there.

"I'm fine," I say. "This place just creeps me out."

"It's super disturbing," Holden agrees. "And you've not even seen the half of it."

"Are you kidding? We have more to see than has been seen?" I groan. "I came here once when I was a kid, but it seemed much smaller then. Is there a secret exit? I think I need some air."

"This way," Holden says with a mischievous smile. "I've got something to show you. I promise you'll like it."

He grabs my hand, and we walk through room after room filled with terrifying circus collectibles, blank-eyed porcelain dolls, and a host of unspeakable oddities that I make myself forget as soon as we're past them. Our hands stay linked together, and Holden runs his thumb along mine absentmindedly, like it's the most natural thing. Like we haven't been broken up for months. Like he didn't rip my heart into pieces.

Like we *had* kissed twice two days ago. Like he might still have feelings for me. Like I could trust him to cash the lotto ticket and give the money to me.

Shit.

What am I even doing?

"Where are we going?" I say.

It's vaguely alarming that we haven't seen any of our classmates for a while, but this place is huge. We'll catch up with them eventually. Or we'll just wander until we have to start making out to have something to take our mind off the millions of unnerving things around us.

I'll take option B, please and thank you.

"There it is," Holden says, stopping abruptly. "Look."

He releases my hand and points upward.

"Holy shit," I mutter.

Above us rises an enormous whale. Its belly is painted black, and its mouth is open, revealing rows of huge, pointed teeth. It's not real, thank God (though I wouldn't put it past old Alex Jordan to have a taxidermied whale tucked away somewhere).

"It's supposed to be fighting a squid, see?" Holden points at the tentacles rising out of the floor to wrap around the whale. He takes my hand again, leading me up a ramp that spirals around the whale so we can see the whole whale-squid battle from all angles.

"This is outrageous and wonderful," I say, peering down at the whale. "I never thought I'd be able to go whale watching in the middle of rural Wisconsin."

"Thought you'd like it." Holden grins at me. "And it makes your sweatshirt that much more appropriate."

I laugh as I look down at my *Whale Watcher* shirt.

"It's perfect," I say. "Take my picture?"

I hand Holden my phone. He holds it up. "Say whale watching."

I stand in front of the giant whale, arms outstretched, grinning. "Whale watching."

He takes a bunch of silly photos and then hands the phone back to me.

"Thank you." I loop my arm through his, giving him a small hug.

"I like seeing you happy," he says.

He likes seeing me happy.

Well. Shit.

Of course, I kiss him right there and then, beside the giant whale, not caring if anyone from our class sees.

"Jane," Holden says in a low voice, pulling away from the kiss. "I've got to ask you—"

But before I can find out what Holden wants to ask, a loud bunch of voices fill the room.

"There you are, Holden!" yells Banks, one of the cross-country dude-bros. "We've been looking all over for you. Get down here— we've got to show you this one room full of old cars."

Banks jogs up to us, taking in how close we're standing and our entwined hands. His eyebrows shoot up, and Holden drops my hand.

At the same moment, a loud whistle splits the room. That's

Bran, with the whistle we've been using since we were in middle school. He waves at me from the bottom of the ramp.

"I've got to go," I say to Holden, suddenly feeling too exposed. "Text me later if you want to chat. And thanks for showing me this whale."

"I'm confident you would have bumped into it eventually," Holden says. "Talk to you later tonight."

Holden waves as his friends pull him away in the opposite direction. I start down the ramp, not even sure what just came over me or what Holden means about later tonight, but I'm looking forward to it just a little too much.

CHAPTER SEVENTEEN

Tuesday and Wednesday speed by. Both days, I go to school and soccer practice, though we barely have a practice field since it's Homecoming weekend and the football team is drilling on half of our field. After soccer, Bran and I walk around town, knocking on doors and "looking for clues," as he puts it.

He hasn't found any yet, which is wonderful because he's no closer to discovering my secret. And which makes me a terrible friend for being happy about, since he's no closer to discovering my secret.

When I get home both nights, I check the lotto ticket—still tucked into *Sea Change*, still unsigned, and I'm still not sure what to do with it. Holden texts me daily, and we chat for hours, though he doesn't hang out with me at school. Which is kind of odd, but maybe we're taking things slowly?

On Thursday night—a little more than a week before my birthday—Bran and I are sitting behind the café counter at the pumpkin farm, drinking steaming cups of cider and talking about our next steps. Well, he's talking about next steps in the investigation. I'm listening and trying to not to check my phone obsessively, hoping that Holden has texted me. We've been slammed all night, but the café cleared out as the last hayride of the day headed into the field.

"The trail has mostly gone cold," Bran says in a frustrated voice. "If we could get access to Wanda's, just to take a look at the scene, then maybe we'd get some new information."

"Did Wanda ever return your email?"

Bran shakes his head. "Not really. I got a short reply that was like, 'Hi, Bran, I'm having a great time at the beach. When I get back, we'll see about helping you discover the lotto winner.'"

"What are you going to do?" I put my feet up on the chair in front of me.

Bran starts to reply, but his voice is drowned out as the bell on the café door makes a jangling noise. We both look up, expecting to see more flannel-clad families wanting cider or pumpkins, but it's Bran's mom. She shoots us a look, and we jump to our feet. I grab a rag and hurry around to the cluster of wooden tables on the other side of the counter.

"It's not break time!" she says with a laugh. "Though, I'm sure you've earned it today. Phew, I always forget how busy these October nights are. Can one of you go yell at the jerks in the corn maze who are throwing water balloons at people?" She lets out a frustrated breath.

The corn is over six feet tall, and in the middle of the maze, there's a ten-foot platform where you can stand and see across the ocean of corn. It's a great view, but, unfortunately, it's also a great spot to lob things at the other people still stuck in the maze.

"Not it!" Bran and I call out at the same time.

At night, the corn maze is also full of "Halloween haunt" actors who are paid to jump out and frighten folks. I scare easily and suspense kills me (I can't even resist the temptation to peek at the endings of most books, so forget horror movies or thrillers). My one-time maze walk-through at the start of the season was more than enough for me.

"You'll both go," Bran's mom decides.

"But who'll watch the café?" Bran asks.

"Me," his mom says. "I need those guys out of there before the hayride gets back so the families can go through the maze without getting drenched."

"Fine." Bran stands up.

"We'll take care of it, Mrs. K," I say as we head out the door.

She gives me a tired wave and doesn't look up from her phone.

Outside, it's a beautiful October night. The last rays of sunset paint the sky peach, and the charcoal-stroke outlines of tree branches make the world look like a stained-glass window. A line of geese fly across the horizon, and the moon rises, a pale fingernail in the east. I love nights like this. As Bran and I head into the maze, we can hear shouts and the splat of water balloons from somewhere ahead of us.

"I hate assholes like this," Bran says. The corn rustles, and I'm praying none of the haunt performers jump out. I will absolutely scream if that happens.

"Hard same," I say as we turn a corner. "What does your mom think we can do? Confiscate their water balloons?"

Bran shrugs. "I guess. If nothing else, we can take their pictures and get them banned for the season."

Against my every instinct, I propose Bran and I go in separate directions when we reach a fork in the maze.

Splitting up means I don't have someone to grab if a creepy haunt actor does jump out at me, but it also means we might get back to the café faster.

"I'll go left, you go right," Bran says. I wave to him as I stride off down the path.

I walk for a few minutes, trying not to think about the lengthening shadows and how chilly it's getting as the sun goes down. The stupid platform should be around here somewhere, but I think I took a wrong turn or something. Voices behind me make me freeze in place. What if it's one of the actors in a serial-killer mask (or worse! A real killer, who could TOTALLY hide in a place like this)? Panicking, I dive into the corn, getting whacked in the face as I settle in among the stalks. I'm not even sure this is good cover, since it's like being in a forest of sticks. Surely the darkness can hide me, though. Maybe? The voices grow louder as the approaching figures move closer to my hiding spot.

Two people come around the bend in the maze, and I separate the cornstalks so I can see them.

Ahhhh. So, good news: It's not a serial killer, but possibly worse, it *is* Holden and Banks.

Should I clamber out of the corn and say hi all casual, like, "Sure, yes, I'm hanging out in the cornstalks, what are you up to?" Would that be the weirdest thing ever? Or should I stay put?

Too late. They're beside my hiding spot before I can decide. Their conversation floats toward me.

"So, you're hanging out more with Jane?" asks Banks. "I thought you two broke up." He holds a bucket full of water balloons, because of course he and Holden are part of the jackassery Bran and I are trying to stop. They probably went to replenish their supplies.

I really should step out of the corn and demand the balloons, but I'm frozen in place by hearing my own name.

Holden laughs. "It's complicated. We've been doing a few things lately, if you know what I mean."

Banks gives a knowing laugh that makes me want to punch him.

They keep walking, and I have to scramble to keep up so I can hear them. Luckily, the wind is blowing so my crunching through the cornstalks isn't too obvious. I hope.

"Are you trying to get back together with her?" asks Banks. An excellent question.

"Don't know," says Holden. "Really, I'm just taking it a day at a time. I'm super interested in the investigation she's doing with Bran. So, you know, I thought I'd get closer to her. See what she knows."

Holden's words carve out my insides.

He's hanging out with me to find out more about the investigation?

I can't help but think back to Monday at the House on the Rock. Was he just playing me to find out more about the investigation? But he hadn't even asked much about the lotto winner then. So, maybe he does still like me a little bit after all?

Not that I even care, but . . .

Ugh. This stupid, confusing boy.

I definitely hate him.

I'm definitely over him.

Totally.

The more I think about Holden's and my relationship, the more it's so very achingly crystal clear why he was not the right person for me. Which is terrible, because I spent the last two years thinking he was *my* person. And I was grateful that I had a person.

But I do have a person, I remind myself. Or people. I have Bran. I have my mom (sort of). I have my grandma. I'm not alone, and I don't need Holden to anchor me in the world.

I know this rationally. But the heart is a wild creature that walks its own path.

Banks scoffs, bringing me back to their conversation. "They'll never find the lotto winner. That person's not coming forward until they're ready."

"Oh, I have an idea of how to find them," Holden replies. He and Banks have stopped moving. I pause too, straining to hear what they're saying.

"What are you going to do?"

"I'm going to break into Wanda's tomorrow night and get the surveillance tapes," says Holden. "Then I'll know who bought the winning ticket, and I can find them. Do you know what I could do with all that money?"

Surveillance tapes?

Well. That shoves all other thoughts about lost love out of my mind.

Banks doesn't ask the questions I'm dying to know: What tapes? I thought there were no surveillance tapes. And once Holden's got the tapes, what will he do? Would he really be able to find out I was the one who bought the ticket? Surely not.

Nevertheless, it's not a chance I'm willing to take. Meaning, I have break into Wanda's before he does.

Perfect. Just perfect. If I wasn't a criminal already, I'm certainly well on my way to that now.

I bite my lip to keep from screaming as Holden and Banks walk away and a cornstalk digs into my shoulder. As soon as they're gone, I set off to find Bran.

I come across him near the tower where, indeed, there are still more jerks with water balloons. Holden and Banks are up there too now, and Holden waves down at me.

"Cut that out!" I shout as Banks lobs a water balloon in my direction. I dodge out of the way, but the balloon hits Bran. Bran swears loudly as it soaks his jacket.

"You all need to get out of here," shouts Bran. He takes a picture of them, while Holden grabs Banks's arm and stops him from throwing another balloon in our direction.

One more balloon flies past my head, but somehow Holden convinces the other boys to stop flinging them. They shuffle down the tower steps, and Holden drops a bucket of water balloons at my feet.

"For you, my lady," he says with a wink. "Didn't know you were working tonight or we wouldn't have come. I don't want you to get into trouble."

It's hard not to believe him, but I just cross my arms and point toward the path out of the maze. "Goodbye. You're banned until next season."

Holden laughs and waves over his shoulder. "Talk to you later, Jane! Text me."

I pick up a water balloon and lob it at their backs, but it just lands on the cornstalks with a splat.

"Text me," says Bran mockingly, as we clean up pieces of smashed balloons.

"Ugh. Never again," I say. Quickly, I fill him in on what I overheard Holden saying, including why Holden has been hanging out with me and his plan to break into Wanda's. Bran makes an indignant noise at the part about Holden's treachery, and his eyes widen in surprise when I get to the part about the surveillance tapes.

"I knew it! I knew there'd be tapes!" Bran starts pacing. "What are we going to do about it?"

I grab his arm, stopping him midstride. "I was thinking we break into Wanda's tomorrow and get the tapes before Holden does. Are you in?"

Bran's face lights up. "You mean, do I want to get more information for this story *and* beat Holden at something? You don't even need to ask me twice. Let's do this."

Before I can say anything else, a Halloween-haunt actor dressed as a zombie carrying a fake chainsaw comes racing toward us. We do the first thing any soon-to-be-criminal team would and start flinging water balloons over our shoulders while running for the safety of the pumpkin-farm café.

HOW TO PLAN A HEIST
PREPARED BY JANE BELLEWEATHER

Okay.

If we're going to steal the tapes before Holden, we better learn how to commit a crime. Or a heist. Or whatever.

Luckily, the internet is full of helpful information about criminals who have succeeded.

This is what I've learned so far:

First, obviously, if you're breaking in somewhere, be sure to have a way out. Sure, this seems like Crime 101, but a ridiculous amount of criminals get caught simply because they didn't figure out how to walk away.

Second, make sure you have a good team. It helps to have someone on the inside, which I don't. But Bran is at home right now doing his own research, so I know he'll be prepared.

Third, go through all the ways the plan could work out and all the ways it could fail, like, a dozen times.

Fourth, disappearing in plain sight or into a crowd is a great diversion. In 2006, four criminals stole $50 million worth of art from a museum in Rio de Janeiro during Carnival. They disappeared into the crowds, and they still haven't been caught.

Now that the Harvest Festival is over, I'm not sure Lakesboro can generate crowds of any size, but maybe if we go when everyone else in town is busy . . .

Fifth, be sure to have enough gear. Depending on what you're trying to steal and where it's secured, you might need ropes, glass cutters, tools to break stone, bags to remove debris . . .

But let's be honest. Getting into Wanda's to steal a surveillance tape might not need as much tech as *Mission: Impossible* or *Ocean's 8*.

CHAPTER EIGHTEEN

On Friday night, everyone in town is at the Homecoming football game. It's the Lakesboro Honey Badgers versus the Carlsburg Cobras. Because we are not a subtle town, every window in downtown is painted with variants of honey badgers eating cobras. Normally, I'd be at the game with everyone else, but alas, no honey-badger rallying cries are happening tonight.

Tonight, Bran and I are heisting.

Sort of.

It's the perfect time to break into Wanda's. Downtown is mostly empty—there are only three cars parked on the street, no one is walking around, and the diner and the hair salon both have signs in the window: *Gone to the game, open again tomorrow.* The sun is already down, and it's dark enough that we should be able to slip into Wanda's unseen.

I can hear the news announcer now: *"It was a perfect October night in a perfect small town. Perfect for a crime, that is . . ."*

Despite my nerves, I laugh out loud at that.

"What?" says Bran in a voice that's stretched thin. We're walking toward Wanda's, both of us jumpy.

"Nothing," I say quickly. "I just thought of something funny."

"There's nothing funny about crime, Jane," Bran says in a cheesy voice, like he's giving a PSA.

I can't help it. I start laughing again. It's what I do when I'm nervous.

"Honey badgers don't give a shit," I reply.

Bran laughs at that and then gestures toward my backpack. "What do you have in there? A table saw?"

"Possibly. I just grabbed everything I could find."

"Hedge trimmers?" He points to the pair poking out of the top of the backpack.

"You never know what will arise during a heist," I say, quoting some of my research material.

We get to Wanda's far too quickly. I mean, of course we do, our town is tiny, but I'm not ready to actually begin the heist.

Bran peers into the darkened window. "It looks the same as always. Except, you know, closed."

I shift my backpack again. We're really doing this. Breaking into Wanda's. The part of me that was secretly guilty of breaking the law by buying a lotto ticket is now fully guilty as soon as we bust in. But I can't let Holden get those tapes. Who knows what he'll do with them?

Thinking of Holden makes my stomach lurch. A great, slimy feeling of sadness, regret, and rage fills me.

Fuck this. No more being sad.

"Let's go," I say, taking a lock-picking kit out of my backpack. "I'll get the door open. That way, you're not guilty of the actual break-in."

I do indeed know how to pick a lock, thanks to all the times I've accidentally locked myself out of my room.

I pull a thin strip of metal out of the kit and slip it into the lock.

Bran steps forward, hand outstretched. "Jane, are you sure? Let me. I was researching lock picking all last—"

Before either of us can show off our lock-picking skills, the door swings open with a little tinkling of a bell.

"You've got to be kidding me," I whisper. "It's unlocked. What if a real criminal is in here?"

What if it's Holden? Of course it's going to be Holden. What am I going to say to him if he's already seen the tape? Will he really be able to tell it's me buying the ticket?

"This isn't very *Ocean's Eleven*," whispers Bran.

"*Ocean's 8* is what we're going for," I reply. "I'm Cate Blanchett."

Bran glances at my knockoff Ray-Bans, gray thrift-store overalls, black T-shirt, and my purple knit hat (in my defense, it was the only one I could find in my closet). He snorts.

I shift my backpack. "Before the Met Gala, dork. When she was just cool and planning stuff out."

He laughs harder.

"Never mind. Let's go. Keep your eyes open."

With a glance at the street behind us, we step through the door. I flick on my flashlight and send it around the store. The beam bounces over metal racks full of chips, making enormous lumpy shadows on the floor. I slip my sunglasses into my pocket.

Bran's eyes meet mine. In his black jeans, black turtleneck, and black snowboarding jacket, he definitely got the memo on how to dress for a heist.

We creep through the darkened space, moving quickly past coolers still humming as they keep drinks cold.

"Weird that we could take anything we want," I say, half to myself. "Want some Cheetos?"

"We're not thieves," Bran hisses.

I scoff.

"Well, not regular thieves."

A drawer slams from the back of the store, making Bran and me jump. My fingers dig into his arm.

"Back there," I mouth, pointing. I lower my flashlight so its beam skims the floor. Bran grabs a snow scraper off a shelf and holds it like a weapon.

"You look ready to attack a very frosty windshield," I whisper, nodding at the snow scraper and his puffy jacket.

"Shut up," he mutters as I cover my mouth, trying not to laugh.

There's another noise, a loud banging as if someone's going through a filing cabinet, and we both stop laughing. This could be bad. If it's *not* Holden back there, it could be a real criminal. They could be breaking into Wanda's while the owners are gone. They could have guns, or there could be more than one of them.

You know it's Holden. I shove that thought away because the truth is, I don't want it to be Holden. I want Holden to like me for me, not for my millions of dollars or for any information I could give him about the lotto ticket.

Ha.

I deeply hate this perfidious heart of mine.

Bran and I tiptoe through the stockroom, past the bathrooms, toward the small office at the back of the store. A light shines from under the door.

"On three," I whisper to Bran. I rest my hand on the door.

"One, two, three . . ." he counts it down. I push the door open, and we burst in.

Dammit.

It is Holden.

He's hunched over a small wooden desk, watching security

footage on a TV-VCR combo that looks like it's from the '90s. On the small TV screen in front of him is a girl in a hoodie and a light-pink jacket, buying a lotto ticket. Her back is to the camera, but I don't need to know that when she turns around, her face will match mine. Or that the ticket she holds in her hand has a very specific, very familiar row of numbers: 6 28 19 30 82. Though surely you can't make out the numbers on the security footage. Right?

Holden spins around as we burst through the door.

"Jane? Bran?" he asks. His voice is full of surprise. "What are you doing here?"

I don't greet him. I don't think. I just slam my finger into the eject button on the VCR. When the tape spits out, I snatch it and smash it as hard as I can against the desk. It shatters into pieces. With one quick motion, I pull the gray magnetic ribbon out of the insides, like a child tearing open a package.

"Jane!" Bran's voice is startled. "What are you doing?"

"That's the security footage from the day the ticket was sold," Holden says. His eyes are wide as he stares at the tape I've destroyed. He looks like he's putting together the pieces of a puzzle.

I don't have time to think about what that might mean, though, because at that moment a police siren splits the night. Holden grabs his phone and his bag from the desk. "Did you call the police?"

"No! Did you?" I continue to tear apart the pieces of tape, as if that could somehow erase what was on it and what Holden saw.

"Why would I call the police on myself? Somebody must've seen you two coming into the store." Holden's voice is scornful. The sirens are coming closer.

"Go!" I shout to Bran, who's standing with his mouth open, stunned into silence by the last few moments. I shove him out the office door. As we run through Wanda's, Holden on our heels, I stuff the remains of the VHS tape into my bag, nearly slicing my hand open on the hedge trimmers I most certainly didn't need to bring.

We burst through the front door as a pair of police cars scream up the street, headed toward us. Holden takes off running down the alley.

"Jane! Let's go!" Bran grabs my hand, and we race off in the opposite direction, darting through yards and past houses, hoping not to get caught.

CHAPTER NINETEEN

WE BURST THROUGH BRAN'S FRONT DOOR, NOT SLOWING DOWN until we're in his room. Drawing in ragged breaths, I collapse on his floor.

Bran lives near downtown in an old converted church, and his bedroom is in a loft built into the steeple tower. Between running away from the police and dashing up the flights of stairs to his room, I think my heart might explode. I haul air into my lungs and glance out his window. From this high up, all of Lakesboro is visible, including the two cop cars outside of Wanda's.

Bran slams his bedroom door. Outside, the sounds of police sirens recede.

"Jane," Bran says, as he unzips his coat. He flings his hat across the room. "What's going on?" He's trying to keep his voice even, but it's not working. He's pissed.

"What do you mean?" I try to look nonchalant. I shrug my backpack off and lay it on the floor. Streamers of VHS tape hang from it. Percy, the orange cat who was sleeping in Bran's room, starts batting at the tape.

Bran grabs one of the magnetic ribbons and shakes it. "What do I mean? Why did you smash the tape rather than let us watch it? What is this strange, gross thing happening between you and Holden? Why are you so distracted you keep forgetting things? Are you okay?"

I let out a long breath. He's right about all those things. But when they're piled up like that, it feels like far too much. I shake my head.

"I'm not," I say in a very tired voice. I cover my face with my hands. "I've had a rough week or so."

Bran plops down on the floor beside me. "You're the lotto winner, aren't you?"

I turn to him, wanting to deny it. Wanting to run out of there or to keep lying, but I can't. Not anymore.

"How do you know?"

"Jane. I've known you since we were twelve. Give me some credit." Bran gently moves my hands away from my face.

"You're a very good investigator," I say in a strained voice. "Yes, I'm the lotto winner."

A jagged, incredulous laugh explodes out of Bran. "You're really worth millions of dollars?"

I nod miserably. "Only if I can figure out how to get someone to cash the ticket for me. Because I bought it as a minor, and if the lotto commission finds out, then not only am I not rich, but I'm also a criminal."

Bran lets out a slow breath. "Can't you just give it to your mom?"

I groan and stretch my legs out in front of me. Wouldn't it be magical if things were that easy?

"Can you even imagine the bullshit she'd buy?"

"Oh my God, it would be so much." Bran scrunches up his forehead, like he's seeing the piles of stuff in his mind.

I nod and continue. "I have no doubt she'd purchase entire thrift stores in one fell swoop. We'd have, like, a barn stuffed with wedding dresses. Or a museum of photo coasters. Or who knows what else."

"Maybe a warehouse full of sad-clown paintings?"

"Most certainly at least a basement full of them."

"And don't forget all the dolls. You definitely need some creepy dolls at your house."

"Shut up," I moan. "Don't ever mention that again, and especially not to my mom."

We both laugh, which drains some of the tension from between us.

"But you could use this money to do a lot of good," Bran says softly. "And get your mom some help."

"I know," I reply. "I know she needs help and this could get us there, but I'm still figuring it out. My grandma doesn't want anything to do with the money, and my mom's not an option. I wish you were eighteen."

"Me too," he says. "What a mess."

We're quiet for a moment. It's a comfortable silence, a familiar one. A silence that feels like home, as we both think our thoughts. "Are you mad at me?" I ask eventually in a small voice.

Bran leans his head on my shoulder. "I'm annoyed—because we could've celebrated together, and then I wouldn't have gone on the news like an ass and said we'd find the winner—"

"Technically, you did find the winner."

Bran laughs. "Technically, yes. Though I don't think I can break the story and use it on my internship application. But, no. I'm not mad. You're my best friend, and this is stressful. Plus, I know you. You need to retreat and figure things out, unlike some of us who go charging in and trying to solve things ourselves immediately."

Something in me lifts, like a great weight being let go. It's a gift to have someone who knows me so well. "You're the best. Are you sure you're not going to kill me for my millions?"

Bran snorts. "Not really my style. Plus, I think Sofie would kill me if I killed you."

"Don't laugh," I say. "It's way more common than you would think. I've been compiling tragic stories from lotto winners, and you wouldn't believe some of this stuff." I reach into my backpack, pull out my notebook, and hand it to Bran.

"I've been reading about those sorts of things too," Bran says. He skims some of the entries. A low whistle leaves his mouth. "Yeah, this is all pretty terrible. Did you hear about David Edwards?"

"The ex-con who won less than half as much money as me; blew it all on luxury cars, drugs, and terrible business ideas; and ended up living in a storage unit surrounded by human feces? Classic lotto winner hard fail."

Bran turns to another page in the notebook. "Oh, this one is bad too: William 'Bud' Post the Third. His own brother hired a hit man to kill him, and he was bankrupt one year after winning sixteen million. Damn."

"It's really terrible," I say, flipping through the other entries. "I cannot tell you how stressful it's been to keep this secret. Like, everyone in town is going to hate me when they find out."

"Not if they don't find out until you're ready," Bran says. "I promise, not only will I *not* hire a hit man to kill you so I can take the money, I'll also help you figure out what to do with it."

Before I can hug him or dissolve into a puddle of mushy tears over what an amazing best friend he is, my phone beeps, letting me know I have a text.

I open it and nearly drop the phone.

"Oh, shit."

Bran takes the phone from me. "What is it?"

"Holden. He wants to talk. He says he knows I'm the winner."

I show him the message.

Bran scowls as he reads it. "He's bluffing. Don't go meet up with him."

I know Bran's right, but maybe Holden has an explanation for all this. Maybe there's a chance it'll be okay? Maybe it's not as bad as it sounds. For the sake of everything we once had, I can at least hear him out. Right?

I read the message again.

"I'm going to meet him," I decide. "Just to find out what he knows."

"Well, if you're going, then I'm coming with you," says Bran. "Moral support and all." It's an echo of what I told him when he first did the interview.

I pause, weighing my options. There's really no reason for Bran not to come with me.

"I'd like that," I say. "Thank you, wonderful best friend. When I figure out how to cash this ticket, I'll give you millions."

Bran smiles. "Don't get ahead of yourself. Let's deal with Holden first."

CHAPTER TWENTY

W E'RE QUIET ON THE RIDE OVER TO MY HOUSE. MY BRAIN IS A whirlpool, churning away with possible scenarios. But there's no use talking about them until we know what Holden knows.

I let out a long, shaky breath as Bran pulls into the driveway. Mom's truck is gone, but Holden's car is already there. He gets out when he sees us, and he even has the audacity to wave.

"You okay?" Bran asks. "You don't have to do this."

"I'm fine," I say. "Just nervous. And angry." I drum my fingers on the dashboard.

"Want me to come with you?" Bran glares at Holden, who's now standing by the broken garden gate.

I take another breath, trying to calm my racing heart. "No. Stay in the car for now. Let me talk to Holden first."

"Fine. But I'm right here. Yell if you need anything."

I squeeze his arm. "Thank you."

"You've got this," says Bran.

I'm not sure I do, but I get out of the car anyway and walk toward the gate. I don't say a word as I storm past Holden and sit down on a clear spot on the porch steps.

Holden is wearing an all-black outfit, and his hair is tied back in a man bun, which somehow is not a terrible look on him. He navigates his way through the junk in the yard and sits down next to me. He bounces his leg up and down, like he always does when he's anxious about something.

"What do you want to talk about?" I say, scooting as far away from him as I can.

"You're the lotto winner, right?" He turns to me, a gleam in his eyes.

"How do you know that?"

Holden scoffs. "Jane. Honestly. It wasn't hard to figure out. You broke into Wanda's. You destroyed the tape. Just be honest: Did you buy the winning ticket or not?"

There's really no way I can deny it. Not since he saw everything that happened at Wanda's.

"Yes."

Holden lets out a long breath and leans back on his forearms like he's been knocked over.

"Shit. Jane. Fifty-eight million dollars?"

"I know." I shake my head, still disbelieving that much money is in the world, much less that it could be mine. Possibly.

"What are you going to do with it? Buy your own golden toilet?"

I snort, aching a bit at how silly that joke had seemed on the lake and how it cuts differently now. "I don't know. I can't cash the ticket because I bought it as a minor, so I'm going to find someone to cash it for me, I guess."

Holden sits up, his body a lightning rod. "I can cash it for you."

I shake my head at that, though, of course, I'd been considering it for days. "Why would I trust you with this? You broke up with me, remember?"

"What does that have to do with anything?"

"Well, for starters, I don't owe you anything. And I thought I could trust you with my heart. Which you also broke. Why would I give you the ticket?"

"But I thought we were getting along again. What about the lake? Or the House on the Rock?"

"I overheard you and Banks talking in the corn maze. Remember that? When you basically admitted that you were just hanging out with me so you could find out what Bran knew about the lotto ticket?"

Holden lets out a frustrated breath. "Did you really think we were going to stay together forever, Jane? We're seventeen. We're in high school, for fuck's sake. Stuff like that doesn't last."

Two years of my life is only "stuff like that" to him? Grrr.

"I know that now," I snap. "But I didn't think you'd go away to stockbroker camp or whatever and come back a totally different person. I thought that during these last few weeks, you were back to your old self, but I can see nothing comes before your rich-guy aspirations."

Holden looks away from me, running a hand through his hair. He has the good grace to look conflicted for a moment, as if he's still trying to decide which person he wants to be. All our time together recently has shown me that somewhere in there is the boy I fell in love with. But he's warring with the materialistic douchebag Holden has become.

"I didn't think I would change either, Jane," Holden says softly.

"Why not be happy with what you have?" I sound pitiful, even to my own ears. Tears rise in my eyes as I think of the questions I'm not saying: Why can't I—or why couldn't we—be enough for you?

"It's not that I was unhappy—"

"You said you were. The night you broke up with me." I swipe at my tears, and Bran honks his horn twice, watching us intently. I wave to him, letting him know I'm fine. Holden watches the whole interaction and waves to Bran too. Bran flips him off.

"I was just saying that to make a clean break, I think." Holden shrugs. "I don't know. It's complicated. I did—I do—love you, but like I told you the other night on the lake, I want more. My family has lived in this town for generations. Everyone thinks that Jones boys will stay in the family business, get married at St. Paul's on Main Street, have some kids, go to family gatherings, and then the cycle will repeat itself. There's nothing wrong with that, maybe, but I just can't handle all the sameness anymore."

My heart cracks just that much more. But I strive to see things from his perspective. Because I loved him for so long, I can't help but try.

"It's okay to want more," I say. "I want more than this town and this life too, but why burn everyone you love to get what you want?"

"That's not what I'm trying to do."

"What are you trying to do, then?"

He shakes his head. "I knew you wouldn't understand. Look, Jane. Give me the ticket. Let me cash it for you. I'll give you five million dollars, then you're set for life."

"How generous of you. What are you going to do with the remaining fifty-three million dollars?"

"It's likely just thirty million after taxes." Holden stands up and kicks at the bottom stair.

I roll my eyes. "Okay, thirty million. What will you do with that?"

He shrugs. "Help my parents out. Our store is struggling right now, and I could either get them out of debt or give them enough money to quit working altogether. I'd give them, like, three million."

"Leaving you with twenty-seven million to play with?"

Holden nods. "That's about right. I'd finally get to live the life I've been dreaming of."

"The life you've been dreaming of since stockbroker camp in July." My tone is flat.

"Whatever, Jane. You can be mad, but you need me. Think about it. This way, you can keep some of the money yourself, and you can use that to help your mom or move to Maui or whatever. And this way, you help me out too. Win-win."

Is this a win? Or my only option? Is this a good idea? I don't know, but I'm too angry at Holden to even seriously consider it.

"You think I want to help you out by letting you live the fantasy life you've been dreaming of for the last three months? So you can be just like your camp roommate, Fenton."

"Finn."

"Whatever." I cross my arms and scoot over on the porch step, getting as far away from Holden as possible, so I can think.

Yes, I do need someone to cash the ticket. Otherwise, it's useless. But is giving it to Holden the right idea?

Holden sits down again, so he's right beside me. "Maybe in a few years, we could get back together when I'm living in New York or you have a house in Maui. Just think, Blue."

Blue.

Short for *Bluefin*.

It's the nickname he gave me early in our relationship because my first name has *tuna* in it, my favorite color is blue, and I love marine biology. And because couples do stuff like give each other nicknames that they might normally hate. I was Blue; he was Marlin. It was ridiculous, and I loved it because it made me feel special.

But to deploy it now, when he's trying to get me to make him a multimillionaire? Low blow.

"How do you know I'd even want to ever get back together with you?"

Holden laughs. "Jane, don't pretend you haven't been thinking about it. I know I have."

He runs a finger along the top of my hand, and I shiver. His touch still does me in. Dammit. But how can I ever trust him again?

"I *loved* you, Holden, past tense. But that was the old you. I don't want anything to do with this new you."

Holden's finger stops moving along my hand. He swears softly.

"Fine," he says. "We can pretend that everything between us is gone, but I'm still your best choice for cashing this ticket."

"You're not my only choice."

"What are you going to do? Give it to your mom? We both know how that will end up." He gestures to the yard full of junk and the porch piled high with stuff.

It's one thing for us all to be thinking it. It's another for Holden to say it out loud, and it makes me weirdly protective of my mom. It's like all this junk on the lawn is her heart and her illness, just poured out for all the world to see. And I don't want Holden seeing that.

"I hate you," I mutter.

"But you need me." He stands up. "Think about it. I'll give you two days before I tell the police you bought a lotto ticket as a minor."

"You can't prove anything. I destroyed the tape."

Holden shakes his head and holds up his phone. "I still have this."

It's a picture of me, holding a lotto ticket. You can't make out the numbers, but it's clearly something I could get in trouble for. Or at the very least something that would make the police investigate and cast doubts on anyone else who cashes the ticket for me.

"So you're blackmailing me? That's your evil plan?"

"Think of it as I'm giving you a deadline to help you do the right thing."

"Fuck you, Holden," I say, standing up.

He cringes. And then his eyes harden. It's like watching him turn from the boy who might do the right thing with the money into someone else.

"Love you too, Jane. Let me know by Sunday at midnight." Holden walks back to his car. I somehow manage to not throw a broken dump truck at him as he pulls out of my driveway.

Hot tears stream down my face as Bran gets out of his car and walks over to me.

"You okay?" Bran asks. "What did he say?"

In a halting voice, I fill Bran in on Holden's proposal.

"Don't decide tonight," Bran says. "Maybe we can come up with something. You want to stay over at my house?"

I shake my head. I'm exhausted and just want to curl up in my own bed. "I'm going to take a shower and sleep. I'll call you tomorrow."

Bran gives me a hug and then drives away. Once he's gone, I try to make sense of things.

So, my ex-boyfriend is my best option for cashing the lotto ticket.

But he's also blackmailing me, so naturally I don't want to give him anything.

But what other choice do I have?

My heart is still in pieces. When does this hurt get easier? Why let anyone close if it's just going to end badly?

This is so much worse than I thought.

I do need Holden to cash this ticket, but I deeply don't want him to have any of this money.

What am I going to do?

"Go take a shower," I say out loud to myself. "You can figure out everything else from there."

Heeding my own advice, I head into my house.

CHAPTER TWENTY-ONE

T HE NEXT DAY, SATURDAY, I SLEEP IN WAY LATER THAN I MEAN TO because I was up half the night, worrying about the lotto ticket.

I stumble out of bed and make my way down the hallway. A bunch of shoes fall as I squeeze past Mom's door. She's nowhere in sight, but her door is cracked.

"Mom?" I call, pushing open the door ever so slightly.

My breath catches in my throat as I flick on the light. I haven't been in this room in years. When we moved back after Dad died, Mom and I retreated to our own corners of the house. Grandma's room was in between ours, and we somehow staked out our own territories. I didn't disturb Mom's space. She didn't disturb mine.

But oh my God. I should have looked in on Mom a little sooner. If the rest of the house is any indication of how grief has shaken her, her room is an intimate portrait of just how lonely and heartbroken she is.

I step inside the room, and it's like stepping backward in time.

Everything looks exactly the same as it did in Mom and Dad's old bedroom from our house in Nashville. She's painted the walls the same shade of turquoise, the bedspread is the same gray one, all the same photos—including ones of me from the time I was a baby until I was twelve—hang on the wall. Mom's dresser is crowded with a jewelry box, photos, and books. Dad's dresser, which I didn't even know she still had, is sitting in the same way it used to, below a window, and on top of it is a half-empty bottle of his cologne and a pile of his books that still have bookmarks in them. Stacks of newspaper cover the floor, and there are boxes all over the room. Carefully, so I don't knock anything over, I walk to the dresser and pick up the cologne, spraying a small bit in the air.

Instantly, my dad is in the room with me. Putting his arm around me after a tough day at school. Taking a walk with me outside and lending me his sweater because it was chilly.

I inhale deeply, wanting to savor this moment with my dad's ghost. Which is, of course, what Mom must do. Putting down the bottle of cologne, I walk toward the bed. It's not made up, and one side has clearly not been slept on. Somehow, there's a space that's exactly Dad-shaped there. Mom must fix the pillows in such a way to keep it.

It's both incredibly sad and a bit creepy.

Moving away from the bed, I open the closet doors. Half the clothes are Mom's and half are Dad's. I didn't even know she'd kept all his things. Why keep a dead man's clothes in a closet?

Because he's gone, that's why. And this is how she can have some small part of him still here.

Even so, this sanctuary Mom has built to him can't be helping her heal. I run my hand along one of Dad's old sweaters. It's dark blue and has patches at the elbow. Surely Mom won't miss it among the other three dozen or so shirts in the closet.

I pull it from the hanger and slip it over my T-shirt. It feels a little bit like I'm wrapping myself in armor. Or in the strength of my firefighter father, who would march into a burning building and try to do something about it.

Closing the closet door, I walk out of Mom and Dad's room—no, just Mom's room—and walk toward my own.

MY PHONE DINGS WITH A TEXT A FEW MINUTES LATER.

BRAN: You hanging in there? Worried about you.

JANE: I'm fine. Just need some time to think.

BRAN: What are you going to do? I'm working all day, so I can't hang out.

JANE: Not sure, but I'll text you when I figure it out. <3

Once I put my phone away, I ask myself the same question: What am I going to do? I can't stay at home and stew all day.

My eyes fall on the *Whale Watcher* sweatshirt that Holden gave me.

Suddenly, today has a goal: find a spot where I can burn this wretched thing. I stuff it into my backpack (after I take off the whale enamel pin Holden gave me; that goes in the trash) and grab my phone and a lighter.

Before I leave my room, I check that the ticket is still in its hiding spot. Yep. Still in *Sea Change*, still on my bookshelf. Maybe I should take it with me? But then, what if I lose it? Or get mugged?

Mugged? Good grief, Jane. This is Lakesboro, not New York City. No one is going to mug you.

Fine. Fair point. It can go with me, and given Holden's deadline, I feel safer somehow having the ticket on me.

I stuff *Sea Change* into my backpack as well. Then I head downstairs, navigating around the piles of stuff, praying nothing new has popped up since last night to trip me.

I stop in my tracks on the way to the kitchen. Where the one wedding dress we found on Big Junk Dump day once hung, Mom has added the other one we found at St. Vinny's. But somehow, that's not all. The wedding dresses seem to be multiplying. Now five more wedding dresses, all in various states of disrepair and decay, hang in the living room.

My house is officially Miss Havisham's parlor. I half expect Mom to be sitting in the middle of the dresses, eating moldering wedding cake and shouting at me. Something about all these wedding dresses undoes me.

Like, I knew Mom was a hoarder, though we never really said the word. And I knew this was a problem—I even looked up why people hoard, and it all has to do with mental illnesses that can be addressed through therapy—but somehow this room full of wedding dresses, which she clearly went back to the thrift store in Madison for and she clearly spent hundreds of dollars on, is evidence of how sick Mom really is.

Would she even let me help her? Is her obsession with saving other people's cherished things and memories really harming anyone? If I don't mind living among her mess and it's not unsanitary, is it that big a problem?

I don't have answers to those questions, and I've got big enough problems of my own. At least for today.

I fill an old pop bottle with water and throw the last granola bar in the cupboard into my bag. The cabinets are empty except for a bag of rice and an old ramen package. I put that in my backpack too. Who knows how long I'll be out today.

Head full of possibilities, I slip out of the house and into the chill of a late October morning. The grass is wet with dew, which soaks into my sneakers, but the sun is out, promising it'll warm up a bit later. Snatching my bike from the pile of other bikes Mom has "rescued," I pedal away from the house as fast as I can.

A FIFTY-TWO-MILE BIKE PATH RUNS THROUGH MY TOWN AND THEN INTO the countryside. The path was carved out by glaciers long ago, and it's one my favorite places to disappear into nature. I steer my bike through town, heading toward the trailhead. I pedal quickly so I don't run into anyone I know. I have my hood up, and there's no reason anyone should recognize me. But still, a raw edge fires my nerves as I turn left at the main stoplight in downtown. If I'm lucky, I won't bump into anyone I know.

But of course, I'm not that lucky. As I'm waiting at the stop sign on Main Street for my turn to go, a car pulls up beside me. I glance over quickly, and Holden's eyes meet mine.

Shit.

He starts to unroll his window, mouthing something, but I don't want to hear it. All I feel when I see him is rage. Whipping my bike around, I head left before it's my turn to go. A station wagon with a headless deer carcass tied to the top (because hunting season in Wisconsin, ew) nearly runs me down. The driver slams on his brakes and honks at me.

I wave an apology and pedal as fast as I can to get off the street before Holden can follow. It takes some darting around town, but I make my way to the bike trail without Holden catching up to me.

And then, as I steer my bike onto the long stretch of hard-packed dirt and gravel, something in me lifts. I pedal hard, putting my body into it as I race away from town. I'm heading east. That's all I know and all I care to know. Above me, the trees are a fire-bright tunnel of orange and red, and the wind makes them creak like ships on the water.

Harder, faster, I pedal, putting every worry, fear, care, and anxiety into the simple motion of my feet. Up, down, forward. Always keep moving forward. It's not a race, but yes, it is. A race to stay away from those who would hurt me. Who would take what I have. Who want to use me for what I can give them.

I skid to a halt all of a sudden, scaring a gray squirrel running across the path. My breath comes in staccato gasps, and I put my feet firmly on the ground.

Is this what it will be like forever if I cash the ticket? Racing to get away? Not sure who to trust?

I take a long sip of water and look around. I'm farther down the trail than I've ever been. My phone just barely has cell service out here.

BRAN: Jane. Are you okay? Checking on you again.

I can't leave him hanging. I could disappear entirely from the rest of the world (well, except for maybe Grandma—I'd send her a postcard), but I can't just vanish on Bran. I take another long swig of water and reply to his text.

JANE: I'm taking a day to think. Heading into nature for a while.

BRAN: You know I hate when you do this, right?

Disappearing into nature is my favorite coping strategy when life gets to be too much or when I just need to think. Before I got the job at Bran's family's pumpkin farm, I'd walk the fields and woods by my house for hours, putting miles under my feet, not coming home until it was nearly full dark. Bran has given me many lectures about how ill-advised all this wandering is, but part of me still needs to move through outdoor spaces to make sense of the chaos in my head.

JANE: You know I'm going to be an oceanographer and will be off the grid for weeks at a time?

BRAN: That's different. You'll have a boat and a crew, not just be wandering the woods in the wilds of southern Wisconsin.

JANE: I swear, I'm fine. Don't worry.

BRAN: Can you hear my long-suffering sigh from there? At least tell me where you are generally, so I can send out a search party if I don't hear from you tonight.

JANE: Why are you the best? Seriously. Thank you for worrying. I'm headed east on the bike trail. I'll text you when I get home later tonight.

BRAN: Be safe. And don't worry about this lotto ticket mess. We'll figure it out.

JANE: Not so sure about that, but if you see Holden, please feel free to shove him into a trash can or something.

BRAN: Will do.

I put away my phone, and that's it, my last contact with another human for a while. Slipping my phone into my backpack, I climb back onto my bike. Not sure where I'm going, but with miles of path before me, I'll figure it out.

Eventually, by the time the sun is almost overhead, I stop. I've been biking for what feels like hours, and my legs ache. Plus, I have to pee. I steer my bike toward a small state park that's directly off the trail. It's not much, just some picnic tables, a bathroom, a small playground, and a collection of fields for people to play in.

At the playground, a family sits around a picnic table, eating sandwiches. It's a mom, dad, and a toddler. The little girl runs back and forth between her parents and the playground, giggling as she tosses leaves onto their heads and then runs away. I remember doing exactly the same thing with my parents when I was younger. My dad would make a huge leaf pile from the old oaks in our backyard in Nashville. Then I'd go down the slide on my play set and land in the leaf pile with a whoosh. I can still hear Mom laughing as she and Dad chased each other around the yard, flinging piles of crinkling leaves in the air. I ran up behind them to add to the leaves, and then Dad swooped Mom off her feet and into the pile. He tumbled in after her, and I jumped in too. Laughter, the crunch of leaves, my parents' arms around me. All the feelings of home.

I turn away from the happy, laughing family before they see me. No reason to creep them out by staring.

As I walk through the park, missing my family is a bone-deep ache inside me. It's a tangible feeling that the wind can't whip away. That nothing can fix. I might have won the lotto, but there's no amount of money to bring back what we had.

That kills me.

I wander the park until my hands are blocks of ice and the wind finds its way into my layers. After a quick trip to the park restroom, I return to the picnic area and playground. The family is long gone, and I bend over one of the fire pits, shoving the sweatshirt from Holden into it. I add a few sheets of papers and then light it with the lighter I brought from home.

The wind takes the first few sparks, and the flame sputters, like it doesn't want to burn. I cup my hands around it until flame bites into the hood, the sleeves, and lastly the *Whale Watcher* logo. I have to turn away as the hungry flames devour everything that Holden and I could've been.

CHAPTER TWENTY-TWO

WHEN I GET BACK HOME, THE SUN IS SETTING. MOM'S TRUCK IS IN the driveway, and smoke rises from the backyard. I can hear Mom out there, singing along to the country music on the radio. Which means she's drunk, because that's the only time she lets music fill her up so much that she'll sing anything. I walk around the house, careful not to impale myself on any of the rusty toys or playground equipment.

Mom stands on one side of the firepit. She's wearing a jacket that belonged to Dad and dancing to the music. Her best friend, Doris, sits in a lawn chair next to the fire, drinking straight from a bottle of whiskey.

"Jane!" Mom calls, gesturing me over. I'm too tired to hang out, especially with Mom and Doris, but I walk over to Mom anyway.

"How's it going?" I ask. Doris offers me a sip of whiskey, and I take it. It burns all the way down.

"Happy almost-birthday, baby girl," Mom says, raising a beer bottle. "I can't believe you're nearly an adult."

She throws her arms around me in a sloppy hug.

I so want to believe this is a safe space. That Mom's hug is more than a drunken whim. I want to sink into it and tell her about the ticket so worrying about Holden wouldn't even be an issue.

But I can't. I don't. That's not how we are, no matter how much I want it to be like that.

"Did you hear somebody broke into Wanda's last night?" Doris asks me. She holds up her phone. "I just saw it on the news. Don't think they took anything though, so the police are dropping the case.

"Really?" I ask in a weak voice. "Wonder what happened."

Mom shakes her head as she lets go of me. "I'm sure it has to do with that winning ticket. The winner still hasn't come forward! What's wrong with them? I wish I had the ticket. I'd buy Storage Solutions."

Doris laughs and raises her bottle at Mom. "I'd give it to you and then take off on a motorcycle to see Alaska."

"Can you even imagine all the stuff I could rescue?" Mom adds. "We'd have warehouses full!"

She and Doris start talking excitedly about everything they could buy with the lotto money. It's exactly what I'd thought would happen and precisely why Mom cannot help me with the ticket.

"Okay, I'll leave you to the daydreaming," I say. "Good night."

"Wait! Jane," Mom says. "Let me show you what Doris brought over." She pulls a box out from between their lawn chairs. The top of a miniature fake Christmas tree and some tinsel poke out of it.

"Mom, I'm not interested in a box of other people's Christmas stuff. I'm going to bed. It's been a long day."

"Suit yourself," Mom says. "We have a whole truckload of these boxes, so maybe you can go through some with me tomorrow."

"Can't wait," I mutter.

Mom beams at me, oblivious to sarcasm.

I walk away from Mom and Doris, not listening to their exclamations of delight as they get drunker and rifle through the boxes. Trudging up to my room, I check my phone. Maybe the whole thing with Holden was a mistake. Maybe he's not actually blackmailing me. But no. The texts are still the same. He's still an asshole. My heart still aches.

I know something's wrong the moment I unlock my bedroom door. The window is wide open, and a cool breeze blows the curtains around. But that's not what stops me in my tracks. My room—my sanctuary, my clean, tidy space—is now a wreck.

No. No, no, no.

It's been completely ransacked, like something out of a movie. Papers swirl off the top of my desk. My laundry bin is tipped over, and the dresser and closet are emptied. My clothes lie in piles. But that's not what makes bile rise in my throat. My books. Oh no. No. All my books have been pulled off the shelves and are now heaped onto my bed.

Where is it?

Desperate, my heart racing, I dig through the pile of books. All my favorite works of fiction—*The Disasters, Descendant of the Crane, The Flight Girls, The Nightingale, The Poet X, The Night Circus, Blood, Water, Paint, The Art of Losing,* and hundreds of others—have been trashed, their pages torn out carelessly. Underneath them are my science books—all the biology textbooks I found at a yard sale and, guttingly, in the marine biology overview from Mrs. Davis, the inscription she put in it (*To Jane, who will go far and explore so much of the great blue world . . .*) has been ripped away.

I shove all the books off the bed and then go through them one at a time, having to read some titles through torn-off covers. *Sea Change* isn't anywhere. Not in the pile of books. Not in the clothes on the floor. Meaning I have no idea where the lotto ticket is.

I move from the bedroom to my bathroom.

For fuck's sake, whoever broke into my room even went through the drawers in my bathroom and all my personal stuff. Makeup fills the sink, and my toothbrush is on the floor.

So. Gross.

Stuck to the bathroom mirror is a small blue square of paper. The handwriting is unmistakably Holden's. Of course the paper is blue. For my nickname.

Jane—I will get this money. One way or another. You have twelve more hours.

I feel like I've been punched in the stomach. I can't believe he broke into my room. I can't believe he tore through my books. I can't believe he thinks this would somehow convince me to give him the ticket.

Was he just too impatient? Did he actually think he'd be able to steal the ticket?

I knew this much money makes people do unexpected things, but Holden has now fully descended into a totally different person.

And I can't even go to the police or tell my mom about any of this because then I'd have to explain what Holden was looking for.

I slump to the bathroom floor as hot tears rise in my eyes. It's then, as I try to fit in the space on the floor between the tub and the toilet, that I realize I'm still wearing my backpack.

And that I put *Sea Change* in there earlier, before I went biking down the trail.

Making a triumphant noise, I shrug my backpack off my shoulders and take out the book. The lotto ticket is still in there, tucked in between the pages.

HA!

Take that, Holden, you piece of shit.

As I hold the ticket, I know beyond a doubt that this money will bring me trouble for the rest of my life. If it turned Holden so completely, what other sorts of violence or madness will it inspire? I don't even want to imagine any longer. I'm just done.

The smell of smoke from Mom's bonfire floats through my open window, and I know what I need to do.

There's no more agonizing over whether I should ask Mom or ask Holden.

Fuck all that.

I'll just burn the ticket, and that will take away Holden's leverage and make my life go back to normal.

I fish the lighter from out of my backpack. It's illegal to burn actual money but not potential money. Right?

Standing at the bathroom sink, I flick the lighter once. The orange flame snaps to attention. It's almost the color of the Mega-Wins ticket in my hand. I take a deep breath. This is the right choice.

Slowly, I bring the fire closer to the ticket.

I'm really going to do it.

I'm really going to burn my chance at $58 million.

I bring the flame even closer.

Will this be a moment I regret for the rest of my life?

Or is this how I free myself from a lifetime of worry about other people stealing from me or betraying me for money?

The flame is so close to the bottom of the ticket.

All I have to do is let the fire take it. In less than ten seconds, it'll be gone. Out of my life. Fifty-eight million dollars turned to smoke and ashes.

I hold it above the ticket.

The flames lick up, hungry. Ready to devour $58 million. Just another centimeter, and it's done.

The edges of the ticket start to smoke, and I drop the lighter.

Shit.

Hastily, before any more can burn, I dip the ticket into the water pooled at the bottom of the bathroom sink.

I can't do it.

I should do it.

I want to do it.

I can do it.

I won't do it.

Yet.

Pulling out my phone, I text Bran.

JANE: I'm going to burn the ticket. That's how to get around all this bullshit with Holden. What do you think? Stop me? Or tell me this is the best plan?

I send along a picture of the singed ticket. His reply comes back almost immediately.

BRAN: Don't burn the ticket.

JANE: But it will solve so many problems, and then I won't ever have to worry about whether someone likes me for myself or just for my money.

BRAN: That's ridiculous. Of course they'll like you for you.

JANE: I think my mind is made up. Though I chickened out the first time.

BRAN: Don't burn the ticket. Seriously. I can change your mind on all this. Let me pick you up tomorrow morning, and then give me a day to convince you that being rich is not terrible.

JANE: How are you going to do that?

BRAN: You'll see. Promise me you won't burn the ticket?

JANE: . . . I promise.

BRAN: I'll see you at 9:00 a.m.

JANE: Don't we have to work tomorrow?

BRAN: I'll talk to Mom. We'll get someone to cover our shifts.

JANE: Okay . . . but what makes you think you can change my mind?

BRAN: I know you. And I know how to stop my best friend from incinerating her future.

JANE: *long sigh* Okay. Deal. See you in the morning.

After I sign off with Bran, I go to the open window in my room and yell over the music, "Mom! I'm going to hang out with Bran all day tomorrow. Rain check on our decorations date?"

"Do what you need to do, Fortuna Jane!" She waves back in a sloppy, drunken way. She's got a rope of green holiday garland draped over her shoulders, and there's a silver tree set up between her and Doris's chairs. As I watch, they open a new box, squealing like kids on Christmas morning as they pull out new bits of junk and add it to the sparkly pile that will most certainly end up inside my house.

CHAPTER TWENTY-THREE

B RAN PULLS UP AT MY HOUSE AT EXACTLY 9:00 A.M. ON SUNDAY morning. He's wearing jeans, sneakers, a Screeching Weasel T-shirt, and a purple crushed-velvet vintage prom jacket. I've also made an effort—black tights, a dress with tiny unicorns on it that I found at a thrift store, and a cardigan under my jacket. I'm not taking any chances after the break-in, and *Sea Change*, with the lotto ticket inside, is tucked into my purse.

"You look nice," Bran says as I get into his car. "I hope you're ready for today. We're going to live it up."

"What are we doing? Please tell me flying to Singapore to stay in the Marina Bay Sands?"

I love everything about that super luxurious hotel from its rooftop infinity pool to its amazing view of the city to its incredible restaurants. I've dreamed of staying at the Marina Bay Sands ever since I saw a travel show about it a few years ago.

Bran snorts. "If you cash the ticket, we'll go there. Today, though, we're going to Milwaukee. After we hit up the bank."

"Milwaukee?" I can't help the slight edge of disappointment. I mean, who thinks of Milwaukee in the same sentence as "living it up"?

JAMIE PACTON

"It'll be great," Bran assures me. "Trust me."

He pulls away from my house and heads toward the drive-thru window at the bank in the middle of town.

"You can't take out five thousand dollars," I say, gaping at the slip as he fills it out. "How do you even have that much money to withdraw?"

"College-savings fund," he says, handing the slip to the teller. "I told you we were going to live it up today. And you can pay me back if you cash the ticket."

"What if I don't do that?"

Bran grins. "Then you can pay me back over time when you have a real job."

I side-eye him for a moment. "This might be considered bribery to get me to cash the ticket."

"I swear it's not. But just trust me on this one. We're going to have an amazing day."

The bank teller slides an envelope full of cash through the window.

"Here." Bran hands the envelope to me. "I got us a spa appointment this afternoon, and I have a few stops in mind. You get to spend the rest of this money however you want."

I open the envelope, gaping at the stacks of twenty- and fifty-dollar bills. It's more than I've ever had, of course, but it's also super overwhelming to just be handed it, like there's nothing odd about it at all. Of course, if I were a millionaire, I suppose handing out envelopes of cash to my friends would be something I could do regularly. Which makes it no less unusual now.

"Where are we going first?" Bran asks as he drives out of town and merges on Highway 94, heading east. "Got any dream plans for the day, rich lady?"

I think about it for a moment, watching other cars race by us.

It's at that moment, after a lifetime of getting rides from other people, that I realize I could actually buy my own car if I could find someone to cash the ticket for me.

My own car would mean freedom, independence, and it would almost make me feel like a normal teenager.

Score one for the benefits of being rich.

"Let's start at the art museum," I say. I stuff the cash into my purse and unroll the window, letting the chill October air rush over me. The sun is really bright today, and I realize with a curse that I've forgotten my sunglasses. "Actually, strike that. Let's start by buying sunglasses for both of us."

"Ay-ay, captain," Bran says with a smile.

An hour later, we pull into an outdoor mall and find a store that only sells expensive sunglasses.

"Bran, these are all more than two hundred dollars," I whisper as I peer at the tiny stickers on each pair.

The salesclerk shoots me a look as I pick up another pair and then put them down again. He's only a few years older than us, but he wears a suit and has been eyeballing us since we walked in, probably expecting us to steal something.

Ignoring the clerk, Bran hands me a pair of gold-framed Versace sunglasses.

"More than two hundred dollars is fine," Bran says. "Today's a lifestyle-lesson day. Which ones do you want to buy? Think of what you want, not how much they cost."

That's like telling a fish to breathe deeply out of water.

"Maybe we can go to Forever 21 and get a cheap pair there?"

Bran switches the Versace ones for a pair of Guccis that fit my face like they were made for it. "Nope. You have to pick something here."

"You know this is how rich people lose all their money, right?" I say, standing in front of the mirror and making faces. "They buy frivolous luxury stuff and then are shocked when their money runs out. Warren Buffet—a man who's Bill Gates's best friend and whose net worth is somewhere around seventy billion—still lives in a house he bought decades ago. His only luxury purchase is a Cadillac every decade or so."

Bran rolls his eyes. "You don't have to spend *all* your money this way. But you do need to know that these things are options for you now. So just buy the damn sunglasses already. I need coffee and some art-museum time."

"Fine, fine," I grumble, but secretly I'm pleased.

It is fun to be in a store and choose what I want, not just what I can afford. I buy a pair of cat-eye Gucci sunglasses in black (they're only five hundred dollars; I'm skipping the limited-edition ones with crystals that cost two grand, because I'm not technically a millionaire yet), and I get Bran a pair of Ray-Ban aviators that make him look like a movie star.

"That'll be eight hundred and sixteen dollars," the clerk says.

I make a strangled noise, but Bran pokes me in the back.

"Right," I say. "No problem at all. Do you take cash?"

"Of course," the clerk smiles like he can't believe his good luck.

I count out the bills, and Bran and I pop our new sunglasses on and stroll out the door.

Okay, okay. I'll admit it: Being rich feels good. And it's not all that hard to get used to.

We get coffee—the most expensive, elaborate ones at the local coffee shop on the shores of Lake Michigan—and head to the art museum next. My breath catches in my throat as we walk into the lobby.

"Wow," I whisper, trying to take it in.

The space soars upward like a cathedral, but the ribs of the museum's movable roof are pulled in close, hugging the building against the wind. It's a little bit like being inside the belly of a whale. A wall of curved windows faces Lake Michigan, so it also feels like we're in a spaceship or an ocean vessel.

"It's so beautiful," I say, stepping into the window wells so my body leans against the tilted glass. "I could stay here all day, watching the water."

"Same," Bran says. "Remember, with your winnings you can buy a house on the water and do exactly that if you'd like."

Maybe I could. The thought stays with me as we begin our tour of the museum. There are galleries full of very old things like a gilded Egyptian sarcophagus and headless marble statues from ancient Greece, and there are European galleries stuffed full of paintings of uncomfortable-looking people in bad wigs.

"'Only the very wealthy could commission portraits,'" I read out loud from the card beside one particularly unfortunate woman who's stuffed into a bedazzled dress. "I suppose I could commission some portraits of myself. What do you think?"

I stand in front of the painting, imitating the pose and facial expression of the merchant woman. Bran laughs and snaps a picture.

"Or you could just buy a painting like this. I bet it only costs a few million."

I snort. "Trust me when I say there will be no buying of art for millions of dollars."

"But you could," Bran says. "That's the important thing. C'mon, I'll show you my favorite. It's only worth, like, thirty million or so."

I make a disbelieving noise—I know art masters are great and all, but seriously, $30 million for a bunch of paint on canvas? It makes no sense.

"Lighten up, Jane," Bran says. "You have that end-of-the-world look on your face."

We stop in front of a Monet painting that shows Waterloo Bridge with some smokestacks behind it. It's done in blurry pastels and looks like it is part of a fairy court or something out of a dream.

I let out a shaky breath. "It's a lot, you know? Not just the money, but the responsibility for it and trying to figure out how to spend it wisely."

"There are people to help with those things," Bran says. "Like entire sectors of the business world who can advise you."

"As long as Holden doesn't ruin everything."

"You could just use the rest of today's money to hire a hit man," Bran smirks.

"Ha, ha, great plan. No. I'm not going to think about him. At least for today. What do you want to do next?" I pull a brochure out of my bag. It's from the rack at the front of the museum. "How do you feel about exploring Lake Michigan on a private yacht?"

"I feel like that would be a mistake in late October," Bran says. "But we can discuss over lunch. I've read there's a very exclusive restaurant not too far away."

"I'm not sure I can handle very exclusive right now," I say. "Let's go get tacos."

"Done."

We leave the museum and end up at a hip taco place that sits in a tree-lined neighborhood along the lakeshore. After tacos, we shop for a few hours, and I buy bags of books from a local bookstore. Bran was right that it's too windy and too late in the season for yacht rides, but I file that away into a potential-for-the-future file.

"Here's our next stop," says Bran. He pulls up to valet parking outside an old hotel in the middle of downtown.

"The Pfister," I say uncertainly, reading the name on the red awnings.

"Nothing but the best for us. We have massages in half an hour, c'mon."

He hands his keys to a valet, and we walk into the lobby.

"Whoa," I mutter as Bran steps up to the desk.

The lobby looks like something out of Daddy Warbucks's house in *Annie*. It has a curved ceiling that's painted with puffs of gray clouds against a bright-blue sky, totally giving all the Sistine Chapel vibes. Marble balconies run along two sides of the lobby. Chandeliers hang from the ceiling, and lots of rich-looking old people sit in the lounge off the main entrance, drinking cocktails in front of an ornate fireplace. The front desk is carved from dark wood, and a wall of frosted-glass windows sits behind it. Beneath our feet, a gorgeous cream-and-black carpet stretches the length of the room. The quiet of wealthy places permeates the room. This building is very old, and a lot of very rich people have walked through it.

"Are you sure we can afford this place?" I ask.

Bran grins at me. "You certainly can."

I am not sure I'll ever get used to that. But perhaps I'd like the chance to try.

We get massages. We do some more shopping downtown (I get three pairs of shoes and a new North Face winter jacket), and by the time the sun is setting, I'm down to just a few hundred dollars.

As we're walking back to the valet stand to fetch Bran's car, a young white woman pushing a stroller comes up to us. She's painfully thin and huddled in a dirty sweatshirt. From inside the stroller, a toddler starts to cry. Snot runs down the little girl's face, and she clutches a purple fleece blanket.

"Excuse me," the woman says, eyeing our shopping bags. "Can

you spare a dollar? I ran out of money for the bus, and I'm almost out of formula. And everyone I asks just gives me dirty looks. Like I'm going to use the money for drugs or something." Her words rush over one another, and she lets out a frustrated sigh. She looks exhausted, cold, and desperate.

Bran's eyes meet mine. I nod.

I pull out the remaining money and slip out of my new winter coat. "Take this," I say, handing it to the woman. "You can get a cab to wherever you're going and get out of this cold."

The woman's eyes widen as she holds the cash. "This . . . this . . . this is . . ." She just shakes her head. "I can't . . ."

"Just take it," I say. "Please. Find somewhere warm for your baby and for yourself." ·

Then I hurry away before she can thank me or refuse the money or the coat.

"Jane," Bran says, hurrying to catch up with me. "You didn't have to give her all the money."

There are tears in my eyes, which are not just from the icy wind blowing off Lake Michigan. "She needed it so much more than we did. It was the right thing to do."

Bran slings an arm around me. "It totally was. And see, being rich doesn't have to be all about buying stuff."

He's right, and there's so much good I can do. It's easy to see that being rich would be incredible, but the real question is still: How do I make that happen? As we walk, the beginnings of a plan begins to form in my mind.

Bran gets his car from the valet, and we start the drive home.

"So, what are you going to do?" Bran finally asks as we leave the city. "Any thoughts on how to cash the ticket? Or if you even want to?"

Before I can answer, Bran's phone rings.

"It's Sofie," I say, picking up the phone. "Want me to answer it?"

"Yep, and I think you should tell her about the ticket. She's excellent at listening and can help us figure this out."

I'm not so sure about that, but it would be nice to have another person's perspective. Even if it means one more person knows my secret. I click open the FaceTime call, and Sofie grins back at me.

"Jane! My second-favorite human in Wisconsin. How are you?"

Her enthusiasm is infectious. I smile back at her. "I'm good. We're coming back from Milwaukee. Say hi to Bran." I hold the phone up so Sofie can wave to Bran, who gives a small wave without his eyes leaving the road.

"So, what have you all done today?" Sofie asks.

I take a deep breath. It's now or never, but trusting Sofie feels like the right thing. "Can you keep a secret?"

She nods, her eyes wide. "Absolutely. What happened? Did Bran finally tell you our plan for spring break?"

I glance over at him and he mouths "later" at me.

"Nope," I say to Sofie. "I don't know this mysterious plan, but we've been living like rich kids all day today." I fill her in on my $58 million secret, our day of spending wildly, and how it felt to give that young mother a chunk of money.

Her mouth hangs open for part of my confession, but by the end her smile is back.

"So, let me get this straight," she says. "You have the chance to be a multimillionaire, but you're conflicted because you don't want to give Holden the money. Which I totally understand, because never Holden."

"Hashtag Never Holden!" calls out Bran. "I want that on a T-shirt."

I laugh at that. "Never Holden, indeed. But I can't give it to my mom, so I'm not sure what to do."

"Why can't you give it to your mom?" Sofie shoots back.

"Because she'd just waste it," I say. "You've seen my house."

Sofie looks thoughtful for a moment. "I think it's worth a try, Jane. I mean, give your mom a chance. Maybe this could be the thing that helps her get past some of her issues."

"But what if she just takes the money and blows it?"

"Then you're no worse off than before," says Sofie. "And Holden won't get the money. If your mom does give you some of the cash, then you and Bran can come see me in Sydney for spring break!"

Bran cheers at that. "That's our secret plan, by the way."

"I love it." I grin at him, but inside, my mind churns.

Can I really trust my mom? Is the risk of what she might do worth it?

The young mother we just met rises in my mind. She was scared and frustrated and alone, and I bet Mom felt that way when my dad died and it was up to her to care for me.

She hasn't been a perfect mother, sure, but I think she's tried. At least in her own way. And I know it's been hard on her. She deserves a conversation, at least. The vague plan I had in mind begins to take shape.

"You're right," I say to Sofie. "Thank you, and if this works, we're totally coming to see you."

We chat with Sofie for the rest of the drive home, hanging up only as we pull into a Culvers drive-thru for dinner. While we're waiting for our food, I tell Bran my three-phase plan to get the lotto money. It's rough, but I think it might work.

"You sure about this?" Bran asks as we drive through town. "If not, I bet we could find somebody else to cash the ticket for you."

I take a deep breath. "No. It has to be my mom. I think that's the best choice, and I'm kind of hoping this can help us through some stuff, you know."

"I hope it does," says Bran. He pulls into my driveway.

"Thank you for today," I say as I get out of the car. "It was magical."

"You're magical, Jane. Don't forget that."

I blow him a kiss as I gather all my bags, slip my new expensive sunglasses onto my head, and walk into the house.

CHAPTER TWENTY-FOUR

M OM IS IN THE LIVING ROOM, SHUFFLING COFFEE MUGS FROM ONE shelf to the next when I walk in the front door. Two more wedding dresses and three prom dresses—gold, green, and purple—sprawl across the couch.

I let out a long sigh as I stand in the doorway watching her. All my fears float to the surface, bobbing around like marshmallows in hot cocoa. This isn't ideal—Mom's certainly not ideal—but I have to give her a chance. Time for phase one of my plan: Give Mom the ticket and have her cash it for me. Taking a deep breath, I walk over to her and put a hand on her shoulder.

She jumps as she turns with a coffee mug that says *Wilkins Family Reunion 2017* clutched in her hands.

"Jane! Oh my goodness, you scared me. I didn't hear you come in."

"Hi, Mom," I say. "Did you eat?"

I hold up a bag full of burgers and fries.

Mom shakes her head. "I was going to, but then I wanted to rearrange some things . . ."

"C'mon. Let's go eat and talk in the kitchen."

Gently, I take the coffee mug from her and place it back on the shelf. Mom shoots me a look as we leave the living room, but she also helps me clear off a spot at the kitchen table.

"How was your day?" she asks as she sits down.

This is so unexpected. Like, I honestly can't remember the last time Mom asked me about my day.

"It was kind of amazing, actually." I pop a fry into my mouth. "Bran and I went to Milwaukee, and we spent a bunch of money on sunglasses, massages, and other fun stuff."

Mom makes an interested noise as she takes a huge bite of her burger. Which gives me the strength to keep going.

"Yeah, we wanted to try out what it was like being rich because—"

Here it goes.

My heart gallops along in my chest, and I swallow some of my fear.

My secret is out in three, two, one . . .

"Because, uhm, I won the lotto, Mom. You know, the $58 million."

She chokes on a bite of burger.

"Excuse me, what?" she manages after she's done coughing. "Say that again, Fortuna Jane."

"I won the lotto jackpot everyone's talking about." I pull *Sea Change* out of my bag and remove the little, orange, slightly singed lotto ticket. "Google the winning numbers if you want, but I promise you, they're the same as what's on here. I've had it for days, but it's not signed yet." I flip the ticket over so she can see it's still unsigned.

Mom takes a sip of water, and her gaze meets mine. "I don't understand. How could you have won the lotto?"

The rest of the story rushes out of me. "I bought the ticket on Dad's birthday, and I don't know why or how, but it won. And that would be great and all, because who doesn't want $58 million, but I'm still seventeen, and if a minor buys a ticket, it's actually a misdemeanor. And the lotto commission won't let me cash the prize, and I might get charged as a criminal—"

Mom puts a hand on my arm. "Jane. Slow down. Why didn't you tell me sooner?"

A strangled sort of laugh breaks out of my throat. "Why didn't I tell you? Mom. Look around."

I gesture to the kitchen filled with junk, the living room stacked even higher with garbage, and all the wedding dresses hanging from the curtain rod above the back sliding-glass door. "I was terrified that if I told you, you'd take the ticket and use it to buy more stuff."

Understanding dawns in Mom's eyes. "We don't have too much stuff," she says softly.

"Mom."

She shakes her head. "We really don't, Jane. All this stuff is important."

"Mom, it's not. It's just other people's junk."

"But it had meaning for them . . ."

My stomach sinks, and I bury my head in my hands. "I knew you'd react like this. Mom, hoarding isn't healthy. For any of us."

Mom's voice is so quiet, I almost don't hear it. "I know, Jane. I know. But I can't seem to help myself. It's how I hold on to your father."

"You're not holding on to him! You're losing *me*. Don't you see that?" The words fly out of me, like birds let out of a cage. "This isn't a home anymore, and there's no room for me in it. I feel like you've buried me under all this stuff, and I have to fight for a place here. Like you don't know anything about what's going on with me or what I've been through lately."

Mom sits very still for a moment, as if what I've said is washing over her.

"I'm not losing you, Jane."

"You are. I'm here, but you don't really see me anymore. You drag me out to do Big Junk Dump day when I have homework or just want to hang out with my friends. Everything—every goddamn thing—is about you and what you want or need. And I can't take it anymore! I miss Dad too, but this isn't the way to hold on to him."

Mom closes her eyes for a long moment. When she opens them again, a tear rolls down her cheek. "I'm so sorry, Jane. I never meant to make you feel unwanted or like I didn't care. There's so much you and I never talked about after your dad . . . after he died. We had a lot of hard stuff going on, and I should've been more open with you, but you were so young, and in pain, and trying to start a new school. And . . ."

"What are you talking about? You and dad were the perfect couple. All I remember is you guys making out all the time, which probably scarred me for life."

Mom laughs. It's a heartbreaking, tired sound that I'll probably never unhear.

"Your father and I loved each other so much, but we weren't perfect. Believe me. Relationships—especially ones like ours, that started when we were just barely adults ourselves—are never perfect. Yes, we met at twenty and grew into adults together, but we didn't always do a good job growing together as a couple or as humans. I could've been a much better partner." Mom twists her wedding ring around and around her finger as she continues. "The day your father died, we had a terrible fight about something that's not even important anymore. We weren't communicating well at the time—we hadn't been for a while—and then suddenly it was all out there. It hurt so much, what he said. And I said so many ugly, horrible things in reply. He stormed away, slamming the door on his way to work. I remember sitting at the kitchen table and sobbing because it felt like my world, my marriage, and the great love of my life was shattering in front of my eyes. All I could do was reach out and try to grab for the pieces."

I had heard that fight—I'd been in my room, reading and trying to ignore it—and I remember walking in on Mom crying at the table. I'd asked what was wrong, but she'd just wiped her tears, saying she was fine.

"Did you ever make up with Dad?" I ask softly.

"Never," she says in a cracked voice. "I was going to send him a text, but I was just too upset. He sent me one, though, right before he went into the burning house. It just said, 'Love you. We'll figure it all out.' But then he didn't come out of the fire. And I never got to tell him I was sorry. That he was my person. That I would have moved the world to see him smile one more time. He was just gone, and my awful words were the last he heard from me. So, I think collecting all this stuff has been my apology to him." She gestures to all the piles of junk still in the living room.

A line of tears runs down my cheeks. "He knew you loved him, Mom. You don't have to keep apologizing. He wouldn't have wanted you to spend your life doing that. I know he wouldn't."

She sniffles, swiping at her own tears. "But how do I even start, Jane? How can I get rid of all this? With every piece of stuff I move or every trash bag I fill, it seems somehow like I'm throwing away my great love."

I take her hand, scooting my chair closer to hers. "Dad is not this stuff. He's just not. And you can forgive yourself, Mom, while still loving him and missing him. That is totally okay."

She squeezes my hand for a long moment and then exhales sharply. "You're right," she says, gulping back a sob. "I'll keep working on it. If you promise to remind me that it's okay to let him go. And maybe help me clean out the house. Slowly."

"I will. Believe me, it'll be my pleasure."

She laughs then, still sniffling a little, and puts an arm around me, pulling me close. It's a real hug, and this time, I let myself lean into it.

We sit like that for a few moments. I know Mom has a long way to go—from what I've read, hoarders can't just give it up all at once—but sitting there next to her, I feel more grounded and more at home than I have in a very long time.

"What are you going to do about this ticket?" says Mom at last, pointing to the scrap of paper on the table. "I think you could have a marvelous life with that money."

I pick up the ticket. "I could, but there's a problem. Right now, one of the only options I have for cashing this ticket is Holden, and he broke up with me two months ago."

"I know, Jane," Mom says softly. "You told me, remember? The day after it happened, when I found you crying in the hallway?"

I had forgotten that. On that day, she *had* actually asked what was wrong, and I'd spilled my guts like a fish being cleaned.

"Yeah, well, it's even worse," I admit. "I thought we were maybe getting back together, which is obviously a mistake because now he's blackmailing me. He wants me to give him the ticket so he can cash it for himself."

"Don't give him the ticket," Mom says quickly.

"I won't, but I need your help for this to work."

"What do you need me to do?"

As we eat the rest of our dinner, I explain phase two of my plan.

CHAPTER TWENTY-FIVE

MOM AND I SPEND THE NEXT FEW HOURS CLEANING UP MY ROOM—yes, I let her into my space, which was both a big deal and nothing at all; and yes, she was furious when she saw the mess Holden had made. By the time I get a text from Holden at nine, my books are back on the shelves, and Mom and I have talked more than we have in years. It feels strange and good all at once.

"Are you sure you don't want me or Bran to come with you?" asks Mom. "I don't trust Holden." She walks me to the front door, looking worried.

I shake my head as I put my shoes on. "I don't trust him either, but I'll be fine. I need you and Bran for phase two of the plan."

"Okay," says Mom. "But call me if you need anything." She gives me a hug as she hands me the keys to her truck. I hug her back, trying to put all the things I haven't been able to say into the embrace.

As I get into Mom's truck, I read Holden's message again.

Time's up. Meet me at the lake, down by the beach, so we can talk. Bring the ticket.

I'm so ready for this meeting. Gone is my fear, anxiety, and sadness. I'm still angry, but since more people know about the ticket now and I have a plan, facing Holden is not stressing me out anymore.

I start the truck and pull out of the driveway with the windows down. This late in the year, it gets dark early, and the stars are already out. A cool breeze whips through the open windows as I drive through downtown. It's empty, and the streetlights make it look like a town in a train set or out of a picture book.

Right as I'm parking in the lakeside parking lot, I get a text from Bran.

BRAN: Phase two is ready.

JANE: Excellent. Go in two minutes.

BRAN: On it. ☺

Phase two is the one that will cut the legs out from under Holden. Tucking my phone into my pocket, I park the truck and walk toward the picnic table where Holden waits for me. He's facing the lake, huddled into his jacket, and the wind picks up a piece of his hair, which he brushes behind his ears. My heart gives one last treacherous leap as I remember his hands on my hip, his lips on mine.

Has it really only been two days since we last talked? Did he really break into my room and trash it? Is there any way to save this, at all?

Ugh. No. Don't even go there, Jane.

I curl my hands into the cuffs of my jacket and walk up to the picnic table. Holden looks up. He has dark circles under his eyes, and I hope he hasn't been sleeping.

"Hi," he says, scooting over.

The table is covered in bird poop and fish guts from people who clean the fish they catch right here on the table, but I settle into a spot between all the grossness. Holden just sits down on top of it all.

Like he doesn't care. Maybe he doesn't.

"Hi," I say. My voice is clipped. I stare across the dark expanse of our little lake. A pair of streetlights cast yellow globes on the sidewalk by the beach, but otherwise, the trees and water are an inky mass, moving in the wind.

"Did you decide what to do?" Holden asks. The lights also accentuate the planes of his face, making him look almost like a statue.

I turn to him then, looking deeply into those deceitful blue eyes. We've already been over this, but my anger at Holden bubbles over. "I did, but before I tell you, I have to know: Why are you doing this? A week ago we were out on the lake, accidentally kissing."

Holden shifts his eyes to the side, looking uncomfortable. "Yeah . . ."

"You were being nice," I push on. "You gave me a sweatshirt and coffee. What happened to that guy?"

"I'm still that guy, Jane," Holden says.

"That guy wouldn't be blackmailing me over a lottery ticket!"

"It's not like it's a little bit of money," Holden bursts out. "It's millions of dollars! That could—it will—change my life."

"Or mine," I mutter. "Even if there's nothing between us. Even if that was all fake—"

"It wasn't."

"Shut up. I can't deal with that knowledge from you right now. You know what the worst part is? I was actually considering giving you the ticket. Like, you're not perfect, I know. But I figured you're eighteen; you can change. Maybe you'd do the right thing with the money. But then you broke into my room and trashed it. That was the lowest thing you could've done."

Holden lets out a long breath, like someone who knows they've picked the wrong course of action, but now that they're embarked, they have to stay on it. "I had to, Jane. I need that ticket. I've got to get out of this town, and I wasn't sure you were going to give it to me, so I took matters into my own hands."

"I want out of this town too!" I practically shout. "But I'm not threatening my friends or someone I once loved to get there."

"No. You've been lying to everyone and sitting on millions of dollars." Holden makes a disgusted noise. "You don't even deserve to win it. Like, what are you going to do? Donate it all to some ocean fund?"

That's exactly my intention for some of the money, not that Holden needs to know it.

"Maybe. But it doesn't matter if I *deserve* to win it or not. Luck doesn't work that way."

Holden slams the picnic table with his fist. "It's not fair. I need the money!"

"You really don't. Your family is doing fine. You have a car, nice clothes, and you'll go to college, get a job, and probably still end up loaded."

"Give me the ticket," Holden says through gritted teeth.

"I won't."

"Do you have the ticket on you?" Holden's voice has a dangerous edge.

He moves toward me, and it's then that it occurs to me that meeting him out here, this late at night, was a terrible idea. But it's not like he'd actually hurt me. Right? Or would he? I thought I knew Holden, but this blackmailing, angry guy? I don't know him. Not even a little bit. He absolutely could hurt me.

"It's in a safe place," I jump off the picnic table and step away from Holden.

"I'm still going to release the information!" he says, grabbing my arm. His fingers dig into my flesh. "I'll do it right now."

I wrench his fingers off my arm. "Go ahead and try, but I've got a surprise for you."

Phase two begins now.

I pull out my phone and open the link Bran sent me. It's a video he just posted on his Instagram. In it, Bran stands in front of Wanda's with my mom, who's looking nervous and excited. She holds the lotto ticket in one hand and twists one of the buttons on her shirt with the other.

"Hi, folks!" says Bran. "You're not going to believe it, but I'm standing here with Joy Lynn Belleweather, resident of Lakesboro and the winner of the $58 million lotto ticket!"

My mom waves to the camera.

Bran goes on, "Tell me, Mrs. Belleweather, what does it feel like to have won the lottery?"

Mom just blinks at the camera for a minute and then smiles. "It's amazing. Like all my dreams have come true . . ."

The interview goes on, but I shut it off. I can watch the full thing later. Beside me, Holden has turned a nasty shade of purple, and he looks like he's going to puke. Which is delightful.

"You didn't . . . Jane. You gave the ticket to your mom?" His hands are fists, and he slams one into the filthy picnic table.

"I did. I'd rather her spend it all on random crap than give you a cent. You broke my heart, Holden."

Holden lets out a high, cold laugh. Like a villain in a cheesy movie. Good grief. "I don't even care," he says. "You were a shitty girlfriend, and you'll never find someone to love you."

His words cut through me, but somehow they don't hurt quite as much as they would have a few days ago. Maybe my heart is healing. Maybe I have better armor. Maybe I finally see him for who he is.

"You're wrong, Holden. I have lots of people who love me, and there will be many more. And even if I don't, I'm more than enough for myself." I start to walk away.

"I'm still going to release the photo of you buying the ticket!" he calls out.

I turn around and shrug. "Go ahead. But it's not going to prove anything. It's just a picture of me holding a lottery ticket. No one will know if I actually bought it or if it was just a scrap of paper I found lying around. And if you release that picture, you're basically admitting to breaking into Wanda's."

Holden lets out a frustrated breath. He knows I'm right. Check and mate.

We have nothing more to say to each other, so I get into Mom's truck and drive away. For the first time since Holden broke up with me, I don't look back.

AT LAST! LUCKY LOTTO WINNER FOUND
BY BRANDON KIM

The small town of Lakesboro was delighted to discover the big lotto winner had been in their midst all along. Joy Lynn Belleweather, 42, has come forward as the lucky winner, and I got an exclusive interview with her. When asked about why it took her so long to come forward, Belleweather said, "I've been thinking of what to do with this ticket. It's a lot of money, and I needed some time to wrap my head around all the possibilities. But I've got a very solid plan now."

Belleweather plans on cashing the lotto ticket first thing on Monday morning, and we wish her all the best as this exciting new chapter of her life begins . . .

CHAPTER TWENTY-SIX

ONDAY AFTER SCHOOL, I COME STRAIGHT HOME. MOM CASHED THE ticket today, and she texted me a picture of the lottery office in Madison, where she went with Grandma as soon as they opened. We told Grandma everything, and once she was able to speak again, she heartily approved of our plan. Mom also texted me a picture of herself holding a giant check, and she was on the news in Madison this afternoon.

Some part of me is a little bit sad that I'm not the one holding the giant check and getting interviewed, but I'm also grateful Mom is handling all that.

I open the door of my house and let my eyes adjust to the gloom in the front hallway.

"Mom! I'm home," I call out.

"Hi," Mom says, walking in from the kitchen. She has two cups of steaming tea in her hands. There's a lightness to her step, and she smiles when she sees me.

"Hi," I say. "How are you? Is everything going as planned? Did you run into any trouble with the legal stuff?"

This is phase three of my plan: get Mom to give me the money legally, and then I can figure out how to spend it.

I drop my bag on the floor. It makes a pounding noise, reminding me of all the homework I still have to do, and that's when I realize that the hallway and the stairs aren't covered with layers of stuff like they usually are. They're bare, and I can see the hardwood underneath in places, something I haven't been able to do in years. I look around. The entire entranceway has been partially cleared, and all the photos are off the wall beside the staircase.

"Mom. Holy shit. What did you do?" I say, turning in a slow circle.

My feet move me into the living room before I can stop them. Mugs, mouse pads, and personalized gifts with other people's faces still line the shelves, but all the wedding and prom dresses are gone, and there's a photo of Mom, Dad, and me on the mostly empty mantle.

"I got rid of some things," Mom says in a quiet voice. She plops down onto the couch, which now has two cushions cleared off. She pats the cushion beside her, inviting me to sit next to her. "Well, I didn't get rid of them. Not yet. But I moved them. So that's something."

I quirk an eyebrow. "When you say 'moved them,' what does that mean? Are they upstairs? In the garage?"

Mom lets out a breath. "They're in Grandma's old room for now. But I'm working on getting rid of them for good. Just moving them out of here feels like a big first step. I feel like some weight has been lifted off me."

It takes the wind out of me. She's right. It's a huge first step.

I drop down onto the couch beside Mom. "But why did you do it? Why now?"

"Well, I was talking with your father last night . . ."

"Mom. No. Tell me you're not seeing ghosts or something." I

can't even process this new stage of her grief. Not when we've had such a breakthrough.

"It's not like that." She smiles at the look on my face. "Okay, I know it's been a bad few years. And I am so, so sorry. But I promise, it's not like that. It's just that when I'm really missing your dad, I still chat with him sometimes on Facebook."

She pulls out her phone and opens up the app. There's his profile and her messages to him. Hundreds of them over the last few years.

"I talk to him on there too," I admit, disbelief making my voice smaller than I expected.

Our messages to Dad have been running in digital parallels for years. They're just missing the person who could connect them. We're like two swimmers in side-by-side lanes, each focused on our own laps, not realizing how close we actually are.

Mom puts a hand on my back. "It's the only real connection I feel to him sometimes. I love these old posts, videos, and photos. Read the last few messages I sent him."

"Mom, I don't need to read your messages."

"You do." She hands me her phone. "Read them, or I'll read them out loud to you."

I make a face. "You wouldn't."

"I absolutely will."

"Fine, fine. If you insist." I can't keep the smile out of my voice. How long has it been since Mom and I joked around like this? Too long.

I flick through the messages. My name comes up many times, along with some heart-wrenching confessions of loneliness and grief that I quickly skim. I pause on the most recent messages, a long chain sent since yesterday.

Daniel, I wish you were here. I've been trying to keep your

memory alive, but I've lost my way somehow. You'd really be proud of our Jane. I know you would. She's grown up to be so much more than either of us could've imagined. She's lovely and strong and kind . . .

A sob catches in my throat. I look up from the phone. "Mom, why are you showing me these? I don't need to read your letters to Dad. And I'm not showing you mine."

"That's fine," she says, taking the phone back. "I just want you to know that I talk about you all the time. Just with the digital ghost of your father. And I think he'd be so proud of you. Like I am."

I hug her then, hopeful that we can make this work. That she can get better and that our lives are really about to change.

"This is for you." Mom reaches into her pocket and pulls out a slip of paper. It has the logo of our bank on it. It's for a checking account, and is blank except for my name and a familiar number—$58,642,129.00—both written in blue pen in Mom's handwriting.

"Mom, what is this?"

She points to the name on the slip: Fortuna Jane Belleweather.

"It's your new bank account," she says. "I'm putting all the lotto money in an account for you. Of course, it'll take a while to process, and taxes will have to come out, so this is entirely symbolic for now. But the money is yours."

I clutch the slip of paper, feeling a huge sense of relief. It was always our plan that she'd give me the money, but I wasn't sure she'd actually go through with it. "Can I buy a car? And maybe get you a new truck?"

Mom laughs. "Yes. You can buy whatever you want. I know it's a lot of responsibility and a lot of money, but I trust you to do the right thing with it. All I ask is that you finish high school. Then you can do with your life as you want. And I'll be here to support you as best I can."

My hand trembles as I hold up the slip. "Are you sure you want to give me all of it?" It was part of the plan, but suddenly it seems unfathomable that all this money is mine.

Mom nods. "I'm absolutely sure. It was your ticket in the first place, and I've got a lot of my own stuff to figure out. In case you haven't noticed." She gestures to the house and the yard. "But I was thinking we could start by unlocking our bedroom doors and trying to tell each other things. Maybe we could even to do some things in the world together."

"I'd like that," I say. And that's the truth.

She gives me another hug. "Now, go get ready. We're meeting your grandma and Doris soon. Doris has been calling me all day, and I told her I'd treat her to a fancy dinner and explain things."

I hug Mom again and then head up to my room. I'm still stunned that the millions of dollars are mine, but I'm also absolutely ready for wherever this ticket will take me.

EPILOGUE

Dear Dad,

I think this will be the last message I ever send you. Not because I won't be thinking about you, but because I'm working really hard to live in the present and look to the future. I miss you. I will every day, and I'll never stop wishing we'd had more time together. But I've got to live my life without you in it, and I'm finding a way to be okay with that. Though it still sucks.

I'm sure Mom has told you some of the things that have happened, but seven months have passed since I won the lottery and Mom turned in the ticket and gave me the money. I'm now filthy rich and trying to be smart about it. I graduated high school a few weeks ago, which was both exciting and anticlimactic. As I suspected it would be, given the fact that the last year has been so weird and exciting and terrible. School wasn't always easy, but people got a lot kinder toward me when they realized how I was going to spend some of my (well, officially Mom's) winnings.

I guess I should tell you what I did with them:

After I got the money, I gave a huge chunk of it to Bran. He's been here for it all, and he's the best friend I could hope for. Then I put half of my portion aside in investments and savings, so I can live on that for the rest of my life. I gave Mom and Grandma both a few million, and I took the rest and gave it away. I donated a bunch of money to Sylvia Earle's ocean fund, and I set up a trust for other charitable donations in the future. I also funded a bunch of GoFundMe campaigns from the Lakesboro Facebook group, paid off people's medical bills, and helped set up some scholarships. I sent Bea and Cheryl, the witch couple I met at the Harvest Festival, enough for an amazing vacation, and I even threw a huge party for my entire senior class. It was really fun, and though I certainly don't see myself as some kind of savior, I'm glad I could at least I could do a little bit of good with this money.

Mom's doing well. At least I think so, and Grandma is keeping an eye on her. Mom has been in therapy for months, and she quit her job at the storage place (Doris was super sad to see her go and also baffled that she didn't tell her about the ticket, but they're still besties). Also—hallelujah—Mom cut off all her grief hair. So that's a good thing. She has also cleaned up some of the house—really, she has. We video chatted the other day, and she took me on a tour. You wouldn't even believe it was the same house as before. (The hallway is clear, and all toys in the yard are gone!) Mom also used part of her lotto money to buy that old abandoned grocery store in town. She's been fixing it up and will open it later this year as a play area, community center, and trampoline park for kids of all ages and their families. I'm proud of her. She's no longer collecting people's memories but rather helping them make new ones. You'll like this, Dad: Mom's calling the center Daniel's Place, after you. Which makes me cry a little bit every time I say it.

I'm living in Maui now—I took the first plane out of here

the day after graduation. Actually, Mom, Grandma, and I came here in December over Christmas, and I bought a condo on the beach. (Just like that, cash sale, it was incredible.) I love watching the sunset every night, and I'm learning to surf. I'm also volunteering at the humpback sanctuary, and I'll start a bachelor's program in marine biology at the University of Hawaii in the fall. Which means I'll move to Honolulu for that, but I'll be back here in Maui every chance I get (especially to see the whale migrations in December and January!).

Mom worries about me, saying I'm going to get lonely living on an island in the middle of the ocean where I don't know anyone. But it's an island chain, and I'm already making friends (including a surfer girl who might be more than friends, we shall see). I'm still pretty wary of dating after all that Holden stuff last year, but I've also learned that no matter what happens, I'm strong enough to walk away from a bad relationship. I got a tattoo on my forearm that says *I am enough*, just to remind me of that daily. Speaking of Holden—he ended up staying local for college, which gives me a bit of satisfaction. Though I'm sure he'll find his way to Wall Street eventually. Also, please know I didn't give him any of the lotto winnings. Not a penny. Though I did get him a yearlong subscription to a glitter-bomb delivery service, which I'm hoping has caused him much distress. Because, c'mon, I'm not a saint.

In case you were wondering: Bran invested the money I gave him, paid off his parents' debts, and has been to Australia twice already this year to see Sofie. Well, three times I guess, since we both went to Sydney for spring break in March. It's a gorgeous city, and we got to snorkel in the Great Barrier Reef. Which was EPIC and a life-changing experience. It made me want to help preserve the oceans even more.

Let's see, what else? Oh! Bran did get the CNN internship, but much to all of our surprise, he turned it down. Since he's now loaded, he's decided to not be a reporter but rather to be a travel writer. He's also taking a gap year, BUT when he goes to college next year, it'll be at the University of Hawaii with me, which should be perfection. He's actually arriving today for a month-long visit, and then he and Sofie are heading out on their global adventure. I'm hoping to join them for at least part of their trip.

Well, it's almost sunset here, and I'm going to sign off because Bran's plane will be landing soon. The ocean is calling to me, and I'm going to take a long walk on the beach as the stars come out and then go pick him up. I can't wait for what the summer will bring, and I'm so excited about everything life has to offer me. I feel like I've finally grown into my name and the luck it was meant to carry. The only thing I'm missing at this point is you.

I love you, Dad. I miss you. And wherever you are, I hope you can hear the ocean and see the stars too. Maybe the ocean and stars are all we can ask for in a good life. Or maybe there's more. I'm not sure, but I'll try to figure it out. I promise.

Love always,

Jane

ACKNOWLEDGMENTS

OH, THIS BOOK. SHEW. I LOVE IT SO MUCH, BUT IT WAS ALSO THE hardest one I've ever written because it dredged up heartaches I've carried for years and because the world changed so radically in the spring of 2020, a few weeks before my debut, *The Life and (Medieval) Times of Kit Sweetly*, rode into the world and while I was in the middle of edits for *Lucky Girl*. I'm so lucky and so very grateful to have had such a wonderful team of people who helped me bring this book into our strange new world.

First, forever thanks to my agent, Kate Testerman, for always being a champion of my work and for answering all my frantic emails with optimism, confidence, and humor.

Thank you to my editor, Ashley Hearn, who loved Fortuna Jane from the beginning and whose suggestions helped shape this story in every way. I will never write a third act without thinking about your insight and guidance.

Thanks also to the amazing team at Page Street: Senior Editor Lauren Knowles; Associate Editor Tamara Grasty; Editorial Intern Sabrina Kleckner; Business Manager Meg Palmer; Managing Editor Hayley Gundlach; Editorial Manager Marissa Giambelluca; Designer Laura Gallant; the marketing and publicity team, including Lizzy Mason and Kayla Tostevin; and the wonderful sales team at Macmillan. Thank you also to my copy editor, Rebecca Behrens.

Thank you to my author friends who have made this journey so much better and who read early drafts of *Lucky Girl*: Lizzy Mason, Noelle Salazar, M. K. England, Jenny Ferguson, Joan He, and Carrie Allen. Thank you for crying in the right places, reminding me to add feelings and setting details, and also for helping Jane figure out what to do about awful Holden. (Glitter bomb! Woot!)

Thank you to the other writers who joined me for events and helped promote my books. I so appreciate your support and I loved chatting with you all: Becky Albertalli, Adiba Jaigirdar, Jennifer Dugan, Marissa Meyer, Ashley Poston, Jen DeLuca, Rachel Lynn Solomon, Joy McCullough, Jennifer Honeybourn and the many others in the author community who reached out a hand.

Thank you to my wonderful street team and to all the readers, bloggers, librarians, teachers, and other folks who helped spread the word about *Lucky Girl*, *The Life and (Medieval) Times of Kit Sweetly*, and my other books.

Thank you to the real Mrs. Davis, biology teacher extraordinaire, who was a light to me in the wilderness that was high school. And thank you to Sylvia Earle, incredible oceanographer and badass, who will probably never read this book, but whom I admire tremendously for all the good work she does. In another life, like Fortuna Jane, I would be on that boat with you studying the oceans and helping preserve them for future generations.

Thank you also to Sadie Rogers, my lovely friend who spent so much time cleaning out creeks with me in high school. Ecology Club in this book was absolutely inspired by our adventures.

Thank you to Melanie Richards and Kimberly Canady for

helping Adam and me get to Hawaii the first time. And thank you to Greg and Kathy Pacton for the second trip there.

Thank you to my delightful children, Liam and Eliot. It is my great joy and honor to be your mother, and every day I learn something new from both of you. (Especially in the realms of *Pokémon*, Sonic, cats, all things dragon related, and drawing lessons.)

And thank you most especially to Adam, my wonderful partner, greatest love, and best friend. Thank you for all the long days of hanging out with the kids while I write. Thank you for always choosing us, for seeing me entirely, and for all the support for this author dream. You are magnificent; I adore you entirely. Let's get back to Maui soon, yes?

ABOUT THE AUTHOR

JAMIE PACTON IS A YOUNG ADULT AND MIDDLE GRADE AUTHOR WHO grew up minutes away from the National Storytelling Center in the mountains of East Tennessee. She has a BA and MA in English Literature and currently teaches English at the college level. While pursuing her dream of being an author, she worked as a waitress, pen salesperson, lab assistant, art museum guard, bookseller, pool attendant, nanny, and lots of other weird jobs in between. Her writing has appeared in national and local magazines, and she spent many years blogging for Parents.com. Currently, Jamie lives in Wisconsin with her family and a dog named Lego. *The Life and (Medieval) Times of Kit Sweetly* is her YA debut novel and *Lucky Girl* is her sophomore novel. She has also published a MG novel, *Farfetched*, under the pen name Finn Colazo. Find Jamie online at www.jamiepacton.com and on Instagram and Twitter @JamiePacton.